THE COUPLE AT TABLE SIX

DANIEL HURST

www.danielhurstbooks.com

Download My Free Book

If you would like to receive a FREE copy of my psychological thriller 'Just One Second', then you can find the link to the book at my website www.danielhurstbooks.com

HANNAH

They come here every Friday night.

How do I know?

Because I'm here every Friday night too.

Unfortunately, I don't get to sit down like they do. I'm always on my feet, scurrying back and forth between the tables out front and the kitchen in the back, balancing plates on my arm and taking all sorts of abuse from frustrated chefs who always seem to be mad at everybody but themselves for choosing their stressful profession.

But they get to relax in this environment, sitting in their seats and sipping red wine, perusing the menu and making their choices, and ultimately, filling their bellies with very tasty food.

What are their names? I wish I knew.

I only have the surname that they make the reservation under.

Murphy.

At first, I thought that meant they must be from the Emerald Isle, but after passing their table several times and failing to detect an Irish accent as they spoke amongst themselves, I guess not. They both sound as if they are from the North of England, so they must have grown up on this side of the Irish sea, but sadly, that's about as much as I have been able to discern.

I don't know their names because I have never had a chance to ask, and I haven't asked because I have never served them. The tables I get assigned to are on the left-hand side of the restaurant, closest to the hot, steamy kitchen, whilst the couple always sit at Table Six, which is on the right-hand side over by the windows. In summer, they get a great view of the countryside outside, but in winter, they just get the privacy that comes from being on the outskirts of the busy restaurant floor.

The Murphy's have always sat at Table Six, ever since I first noticed them frequenting these premises six months ago. That's one part of their routine. The other is that they always come on a Friday night, and one thing is for sure, that means they get to begin their weekend in a more enjoyable manner than I do.

Working in hospitality means that the concept of weekends doesn't really apply to me. I'm used to having my time off on Mondays and Tuesdays, those boring, soulless days when everyone else is at work, and there's very little for me to do but catch up on my dry cleaning, wander around the deserted town centre and count down the hours to my next shift while watching dreadful television.

I don't get to go out and party with my friends when I'm working weekends.

I don't get to drink all day on Saturday and sleep all day on Sunday.

And I don't get to go for a romantic meal with my husband on a Friday evening and see the glint from the diamond ring on my left hand in the window by my table.

I wonder how long the Murphys have been married. They look to be in their early forties, so it could have been a while since they said their vows in front of their loved ones. But there's another thing that makes me suspect that the honeymoon period was a long time ago. It's because in all the time I have been watching them, I have not seen much in the way of affection.

They talk to each other, sure, and I have seen each of them laugh at a joke the other made. But I have never caught a glimpse of their hands reaching across the table or their feet rubbing against the legs of the other beneath it. They come in, they eat, and then they leave. It's more routine than romance. But then again, what do I know about romance? I have a boyfriend, but our relationship is far from perfect. There's no diamond on my finger, that's for sure, and while I'm not quite as old as Mrs Murphy yet, I am nearing forty, and I feel like my internal clock is ticking louder with each passing day. But this isn't about me, at least not yet anyway. It's about that couple at Table Six and how I have slowly but surely become obsessed with them ever since I saw them.

I'd like to blame it on the fact that I see them every seven days. Perhaps if they had just come in here once and then vanished, never to be seen again, then I would have forgotten about them. But their names are always in the reservation book on the front desk at the same time every week.

Murphy – 19:30 – T6.

I can see them over there by the window now. Him in a smart blue shirt and grey jeans that make him look very trendy for his age. Her in a pretty pink blouse and black trousers that accentuate every one of her impressive curves. I envy her look and not just because she is slimmer than me. It's because she gets to beautify

9

herself every Friday, while I end up standing here looking like a hot, sweaty mess.

My white uniform looks pristine when I put it on before every shift, but it doesn't look that way an hour into it, once the first signs of sauce splashes become evident. Seriously, why did the manager here decide that white was the best colour for his staff to wear? What could possibly go wrong when we have to carry plates of tomato-based products back and forth all night? Of course, we're not supposed to spill any of the food on ourselves in between the kitchen and the tables, but accidents happen. The small but unsightly splodge of bolognese sauce on my left sleeve is a testament to that.

Along with my god-awful uniform, I have to scrunch my mousey-brown locks into a bobble so that I don't get my hair in any of the food, and while that is practical, it doesn't do anything to enhance my appearance. Add into that the fact that I'm carrying several stubborn pounds around my midriff despite being on my feet for most of my working week, and I can safely say that I do not look anywhere near as attractive as Mrs Murphy does.

I guess that's why I've never caught Mr Murphy looking in my direction.

One way in which it would be impossible for him not to notice me would be if I got to serve him his food and drink one Friday night. But that seems to be a job saved for the younger, prettier waitresses here, and there are plenty of them. I'm the oldest member on the front of house team by far. The rest of my colleagues are nearly twenty years my junior, and not only are they all annoyingly and alluringly attractive, but they also have irritatingly young names too, like Chrissy, Tory and Becki with an I.

None of the guys in here are looking at me whenever Becki walks by in the parts of her uniform that are clearly two sizes too small for her.

It's Becki who is serving the Murphys tonight, and I can see her over there now, fluttering her eyelashes at the man of the table as she pours him another red wine. She's obviously only doing it because she wants him to leave a big tip at the end of the meal, but it's pretty clear that it's working because Mr Murphy looks very happy with the service he is getting from his nineteen-year-old waitress. Mrs Murphy doesn't seem quite so enamoured with Becki, but she must be used to her husband's wandering eyes because she doesn't scold him once the teenager leaves, opting instead to just take another big bite from the slice of garlic bread on her plate.

I don't smile at Becki as she walks past me on the way into the kitchen, and she doesn't smile at me either, but that's okay because we're not friends. I'm not friends with anybody here. I just turn up, do my job and go home again.

That reminds me, I should probably go check on Table Twelve.

Meandering my way through the myriad of tables on this side of the restaurant, I eventually reach the solitary thirty-something-year-old male at T12 and ask him if he is finished with his meal. He looks a little startled when he hears my voice, almost as if he wasn't expecting to be spoken to by anybody in here this evening, but he soon composes himself and nods his head.

'Was everything okay?' I ask him as I pick up his empty plate, and he tells me that it was, although the lack of food he left had already told me that before he uttered a word. But being a good waitress isn't just about carrying plates and pouring drinks, it's also about interacting with the patrons and making them feel like they are the most important people in the room.

So, would I class myself as a good waitress? Not really. I just do enough to get by, which is how I've tended to operate in all areas of my life. I don't excel, I just exist, but I must be doing something right here because Francesco, the hot-tempered Italian who runs this place, has not got rid of me yet. I've worked under him since he took over from the last angry Italian man to manage here, and while I'm sure he would have preferred that I was as young and bountiful as the other waitresses on the books, I have never given him a good reason to get rid of me.

I don't drop plates, and I don't spill wine, and best of all, I never ask for time off. Unlike my younger colleagues, I actually adhere to the rota, and I don't swap shifts like children swap sweets on a playground. I'd like to say that's because I'm a model professional, but it's simply because I don't have a life like the other waitresses do. There are no parties for me to try and go to, nor are there any hangover days that could cause me to call in sick. This job is pretty much all I have going for me - well, that and my boyfriend, but he works a lot, and my unsociable hours don't help there either.

As I leave Table Twelve and the lonely man occupying it, I check the clock above the bar and see that there are still two hours to go of my shift this evening. But that's okay. There's no rush to get out of here. I could hang around all night if I had to, and I'd be more than happy to do so if the Murphys were here with me.

After disposing of the dirty plate in the kitchen and taking an earful of abuse from a chef who blames me for him burning himself on the next plate I need to carry, I return to the main floor and continue with my duties in a quiet but polite fashion. As Italian restaurants go, this isn't a bad one. But it's not a great one, which is why I suspect I've managed to stay employed as a waitress here for so long.

It's just okay. Popular enough to be at least half full on the quieter weeknights and nearly always fully booked on the weekends. Of course, being an Italian restaurant, it needs a name that befits that Central European country and allows its patrons to forget that they are actually in a fairly non-descript town in Northern England. The owner of this restaurant went with *San Bella*, which translates as 'Saint Beautiful' for anyone who wants to know. I guess that is a pretty name, and I have seen several people having their photo taken beside the large sign at the front door on their way in and out over the years.

Instagram filters love *San Bella.*

But you won't catch me taking selfies here. I dread to think what I look like now as I feel a few beads

13

of sweat on my forehead. I'm hot, I'm tired, and I'm needed back in the kitchen again because one of the chefs has apparently forgotten to furnish me with the sauce that should have gone out with that last plate.

What a job.

It would be more fun to be sitting at the tables rather than serving them.

It would be more fun to be sitting at Table Six.

NADINE

That's another Friday night at *San Bella* over and done with. As always, we arrived at 19:30; as always, we sat at Table Six; and as always, we decided to start with a glass of red wine while we perused the menu. But that wasn't where the traditions ended. Like I always do, I pretended to think about it before I opted for the tagliatelle. Like always, my husband, Max, ogled the pretty waitress while ordering his pasta dish. And as always, I pretended not to be bothered by his wandering eyes. Then we departed shortly before ten, Max leaving a twenty-pound note on the table as a tip for Becki while I busied myself with ordering an Uber on my phone. Now we are in our taxi, and we are headed for home, and once we get there, that will be it for another week.

Max will go back to working on his busy business and staying away from home for the majority of the next seven days while I will entertain myself by keeping the house tidy and snooping at my children's lives on social media. But before we both know it, Friday will come around again, and we will put on our finest clothes and return to the Italian restaurant that has become our favourite ever since we first set foot inside it six months ago.

'What did you think of the food this week?' Max asks me as our driver shuttles us down another dark street.

'It was fine,' I reply while suspecting my husband is just making conversation rather than suggesting standards have slipped at our most frequent haunt.

'The wine wasn't as good as last week.'

'I told you to get that bottle of Bordeaux.'

'I know, but I fancied the Merlot. They're usually much nicer than that.'

'Well, you can have the Merlot next week, can't you?'

'I will.'

I wonder if the taxi driver is internally cursing his luck for his latest fare being for two privileged passengers who have no greater worries in the world this evening than the expensive bottle of wine they consumed over dinner. But he doesn't say anything, and it's up to me to fill the silence in the vehicle a few seconds later.

'Those waitresses seem to be getting younger by the week.'

'Are they? I hadn't noticed.'

I roll my eyes at my husband's pathetic attempt at pretending he wasn't gawking at all the wait staff who were half his age, but he sticks to his story and shrugs. At least he only looks and doesn't touch. The last thing our marriage needs is him to start an affair. Max is a red-blooded male, and he likes to let his eyes linger on things he shouldn't be looking at from time to time, but he's faithful, and I guess that's the most important thing.

It's certainly more than can be said for me.

Shifting in my seat because the memory of what I once did has suddenly caused me to feel uncomfortable, I turn away from the man sitting beside me and look out at the field on the other side of the window. We're leaving town behind now and heading out into the countryside, and that is where we will find the home we purchased here just under a year ago. With Max's business going from strength to strength, it was time for us to reap the rewards of all his hard work, and we chose to do that by buying a property that was double the size of our last house.

On the face of it, it seemed unnecessary, especially because our two children had recently flown the nest and halved the number of people occupying the family home. And I'm still not convinced we needed the space for the potential tennis court either. But we went ahead and put our offer in, and it was a very proud day when we received the keys.

Max has always been the main breadwinner in our relationship, but things really went to another level when he came home one day and told me that he had an idea for a new type of filter on an air-conditioning system. Being a mechanical engineer meant that it wasn't strange for me to hear my husband talk about cooling systems and ways to make them more efficient. But what was different that time was that he wasn't just talking about something he was doing for his employer.

He was talking about something he was going to do himself.

Fast forward four years since that initial spark of an idea, and now Max is the CEO of the company that he founded to sell his new filter to offices, hotels and homes all around the UK. To say things went well in the early stages would be putting it mildly, and yes, I am now a millionaire's wife, thank you very much.

But it's not quite as perfect as it sounds. We have the big house and the expensive car on the driveway, but besides that, we don't exactly live to our means. There have been no exotic holidays for us for a long time, nor are we always wining and dining in the best restaurants the big cities have to offer. That's because Max is so busy pushing his ingenious product into new markets and expanding the business that we barely have the time to enjoy the fruits of his labour. I know he has to do it, and I am very proud of his endeavours, but I wouldn't be lying if I said I wish he was around more. It's not good for the health of any relationship if the two people in it spend most of the week in different places, but that's just the way it is with us.

It's also why our Friday nights are so important.

I haven't handed out many non-negotiables to Max since our marriage began. Just the obvious ones like no cheating, no abuse and no leaving the toilet seat up every time he frequents the bathroom. But I made an addition to that small list half a year ago after our first visit to *San Bella* went so well. I told him that no matter what he was doing all week and no matter how busy he was, he had to be home so we could have a date night on Friday.

I'm pleased to say that Max has kept his word since that evening, and so far, we have not missed a single date night at our favourite restaurant. Why do we like *San Bella* so much? Well, I know why Max likes it, but I've had enough of thinking about those waitresses and their tight uniforms. The reason I like it so much is because of the ambience of the place. The décor, the lighting and the music are perfect and always put me at ease whenever I walk through the front door and see all those tables with the white linen cloths hanging over them. With the flames from the candles flickering, the wine glasses gleaming, and the smells from the kitchen sensational, it all adds up to being a very enjoyable place to have a meal and start the weekend.

This week's edition might be over now, but I'm already counting down the days until next time we get another taste of Italy in this part of England.

'Here you go,' the otherwise mute driver says as he parks his vehicle outside our stately home ten minutes later, and Max thanks him as I open my door and place a heel down on the gravel driveway that leads to our front door.

I'm staggering a little as I make my way to the door, but it has less to do with the drinks I consumed this evening and more to do with my choice of footwear. A gentleman would give me a hand in getting inside, but while Max is a polite man, as evidenced by what he just said to the taxi driver, he is not a particularly affectionate man.

At least not these days anyway.

Is it normal for couples who have been married for seventeen years to lose the intimacy? I'm not sure. All I do know is that Max and I are nowhere near as close as we once were. Forget ripping each other's clothes off at the sight of one another anymore. These days, we can barely bring ourselves to pick up an item of clothing that the other might have discarded on their way to the wash basket in the bedroom. It's not that I'm no longer attracted to the man I married, nor is it that I have let myself go and lost the lustful look from the eye of my husband. It's just that being together has become routine, and unlike our Friday night tradition, not all routines are good.

We sleep side by side but no longer snuggle. He pecks me on the cheek instead of kissing me on the lips when he leaves to disappear on his business trips for days on end. And I stopped putting kisses at the end of my text messages to him a long time ago. We're comfortably uncomfortable with each other these days.

But am I complaining? Of course not. I still love him, and I certainly love the life he has given me. But most of all, I love the children we have raised together. Sophie and Adam are the real lights of our lives, and they kept us together all this time because neither of us would ever do anything to break up the family unit we have.

Sadly, our children grew up too fast, as many others do, and now they are getting on with the first part of their adult lives. Sophie is twenty-one and has just embarked on what she hopes will be a very long and very exhilarating tour around Southeast Asia. Meanwhile, Adam is eighteen and just beginning a three-year stint at Loughborough University, where he is studying to be a sports journalist. I couldn't be prouder of the pair of them and am just grateful that they have grown to be two healthy, happy souls.

I miss them terribly, of course, and like most mothers, I wish they would do a better job of keeping in touch while they are away, but I know they are safe and having fun, and that is the main thing. I will keep the home fires burning while they are away, just as I do for Max every time he pecks me on the cheek and grabs his suitcase before hopping behind the wheel of his Jaguar and venturing off on what he hopes will be another lucrative business trip.

With my head full of wistful thoughts, I barely notice that Max has wasted no time in getting the front door unlocked, and once I've followed him in, I waste just as little time in getting my heels off.

'That's better,' I say as I place my bare feet down on the hardwood floor in our hallway and hang my jacket on the hook at the bottom of our very grand staircase.

I might have lived here for a while now, but this house never fails to make me smile every time I arrive at it and remind myself of where I call home these days. I know Max loves it too, and it's just a shame he doesn't get as much time to enjoy these surroundings as I do during the year.

'I fancy a nightcap,' he says as he unbuttons the top of his shirt and heads for the kitchen.

'I might go up,' I call after him, feeling more in the mood for my bed rather than something fizzy from the fridge.

'No worries,' he mutters as he disappears, and I plod up the stairs towards the bedroom, trying not to feel too guilty about calling it a night but struggling because I should probably stay up late and sit with him while he has his drink. But I'm tired, I'm overly full from all the food and most of all, I'm worried that my husband might get a little frisky with one more drink inside him. If I go up now, then I can be asleep by the time he retires to bed beside me, and while that might not be fair, it is a fact.

His birthday is coming up soon, so I'll save the sex for then.

Like I said, we have our routines.

Abstinence is now almost as common in this marriage as Italian appetisers on a Friday night.

HANNAH

I complete my shift as I always do, changing in the bathroom so that I don't have to wear my waitress uniform for a second longer than is necessary. Feeling better to be back in more comfortable clothing, I leave the bathroom and head down the corridor in the direction of the door that will take me out of here. I pass several other colleagues as I go, some in their chef whites, others in uniforms just like the one I discarded, but I don't get much in the way of conversation from them. We're all as tired as each other and all just as eager to get out and salvage something of our Friday night. But while some of these people might be hoping to catch last orders in the local pub or maybe even join the queue at a nightclub that is open long into the night, I have far less exciting plans.

I'm going to go to the nearest takeaway, and I'm going to order myself a big serving of cheesy chips.

I'm harbouring a little guilt as I step out into the fresh air and feel the cold wind blowing in my face as I cross the restaurant car park. It's guilt because I know I shouldn't be seeking out such fatty food at this time of the day. I should just go home, get to sleep and survive on the calories I already consumed earlier. The salad I had before my shift began was supposed to be enough.

Yeah, enough if I was some skinny supermodel who got paid to live on lettuce leaves and fresh air.

Alas, my stomach was growling at me for the last couple of hours of my shift, and now all I can think about is stuffing my face with some food that will do nothing for my waistline but will at least do something for my mood. I'm feeling fed up, which is familiar, and only something sinful will perk me up now.

Crossing the street, I avoid the numerous puddles sitting on the wet tarmac and hurry along on my way, wrapping my coat around myself because it's freezing, and I have no other way to warm up. I'm not going to take a taxi because that would be a waste of the money I worked so hard to earn tonight. It's a ten-minute walk, and I'll just have to put up with it. The chips will be purchased out of the £14.28 I made in tips. That was my share after the funds had been divvied up between all the staff on duty tonight. But I know for a fact that Becki made more than that because I saw her swooping in on the Murphys' table just after they left, and I bet that was because there was a twenty-pound note sitting there to be collected.

I've long suspected some of the other waitresses aren't sharing the money as they should be, but I'm not bothered enough to kick up a fuss about it. I'm just grateful to have a job. And I'll be even more grateful when I have a tray of chips in my hand.

I pass a couple who look like they have spent the night in one of the pubs around here because he is swaying, and she is shouting. They're having a fight, and I wonder what happened as I look over my shoulder at the pair of them walking away. Did he not give her enough attention this evening? Did he give someone else too much attention? Or is she just not doing a good job of handling her alcohol and taking out her tipsiness on him?

Who knows, and who cares? They aren't worried about me, so why should I worry about them?

But I am worried about the Murphys. Did they have a good night? What did they talk about? And did they notice me watching them during their meal? I'm also intrigued as to what they are up to now after I saw them leave the restaurant. Have they gone out for more fun, or are they already home? What are they up to? Are they chatting, drinking, making love?

One thing is for sure.

They aren't going to be in this takeaway.

Reaching my destination, my eyes are dazzled by the bright lights of the venue's flashing neon sign that is doing its best to draw in the drunk and the desperate.

Pizza baby! is the name of this 'classy' establishment, but don't let the name fool you. The guys in the kitchen here don't just limit their culinary skills to circular dough bread with pepperoni toppings. They can cook kebabs, chicken wings and anything else a person might need to ensure they increase their odds of having a heart attack in the next few hours. But I will make do with a portion of chips, and I let that be known to Mario, the guy who operates the till in this place but also doubles as a 'ladies man' in his spare time.

'Hey, look who it is. My favourite customer! Where have you been? I've missed you!'

I roll my eyes and offer a weary smile to be polite, but I do wish we didn't have to go through this charade every time I come here. I know I'm not Mario's favourite customer because I've seen some of the other women who frequent this place, and they are a damn

25

sight sexier than I am. But I do have female body parts, and that seems like all it takes for this enthusiastic Turkish man to be enamoured with me.

'Here you go,' I say as I offer him the £3.50 for his till, but he is in no rush to take it. Instead, he is more interested in showing me his new watch.

'Look. The hands are Cupid's arrows, and the numbers are hearts. You like?'

It's cheap, gaudy and certainly not as romantic as he thinks it is, but I tell him that I do like it because I presume that will get me my chips quicker. Mario is thrilled to get my seal of approval and takes my money then but continues jabbering away, telling me where he bought the watch and confirming my suspicions that it is nothing but a dodgy fake.

He got it at the market, and nothing at the market is what it seems.

'What are you doing tonight? We could party after I'm finished here.'

Mario is trying his luck with me, even after I've walked away from the counter and sat down at one of the sticky tables to wait for my food. But I can't blame him. He's tried before, and he almost got lucky. That was a low point in my life, but I admit I did almost go home with him. I was single back then, and you could say that I was somewhat desperate. But I came to my senses at the last minute and left him with nothing more than a peck on the cheek, which I'm glad about because I have a feeling that if Mario ended up in my bed, then I would have a very hard time getting him out of it.

'No party for me tonight, Mario. I'm going home.'

'I come with you.'

'No, thank you.'

'Why not?'

'I have a boyfriend.'

'Forget about him.'

I laugh at the Turkish man's confidence and almost wish I could be as nonchalant about things as he is. He does seem happier than me, yet we both seem to have pretty lame jobs. Then again, attitude is everything, and he seems to be making the most of his situation, hitting on the customers and amusing himself as much as others. I, on the other hand, get through my working day in a much less enthusiastic fashion, but everyone is different, and we can't all be womanisers from Western Europe, can we?

'Maybe some other time,' I tell Mario to appease him, and that seems to do the trick because he gives me a wink before going to check on my chips.

I check my phone for messages as I wait, but there are none. No friends asking me how my day was or wondering if I would like to go for a drink soon. No family members wanting to know when I am coming around for dinner again because I haven't spoken to any of my relatives in years. And there's no message from my boyfriend either, but that's standard for him because he's always so busy, and I'll see him soon. But with little else to occupy me on my mobile, other than some lame game that a woman my age should not be playing, I put my device away and let out a sigh.

'Cheesy chips!'

I vacate my seat at Mario's call and gratefully accept the hot tray of fatty food before picking up one of the plastic forks from the container on the counter and turning for the door.

'Thank you!' I say as I go to leave, but my progress is delayed temporarily by three teenage girls entering. Barely eighteen with too much make-up and not enough clothing, they don't even acknowledge my existence as they waltz past me in pursuit of their own food.

It seems Mario has already forgotten about his love for me because he is now running his 'routine' on his latest customers, but that's fine by me as I leave them all to it and step back onto the street.

The warmth from the tray in my hands does me a few favours as I walk down the last couple of streets until making the final turn that will take me to my front door. When I get there, I find the house cold and uninviting, just like I left it, but there's no time for turning on too many lights or bringing the boiler into action via the central heating system. Instead, I just sit down on the carpet in the living room and start eating my unhealthy meal, using only the light from the window behind me to allow me to see what I'm doing.

The chips go down easily, as I knew they would do, and while they don't alleviate my guilt, they certainly alleviate my hunger. With my belly fuller than it was five minutes ago, I decide it's time for bed because it's been a long day, and I have another one just like it tomorrow.

Crawling onto the duvet in the main bedroom, I think about sending my boyfriend a goodnight text. But I decide against it because I'll see him before my next shift. Until then, I'll have to make do with being by myself, and I snuggle down under my duvet with the hope of getting some much needed rest.

Just before I drift off, I think about the Murphys one more time and wonder what they have planned for this weekend. I only know what they get up to on a Friday night, but I long to know how they fill the other six days of the week. I bet it's all very fun and glamorous. Maybe I'll find out one day.

I can't linger on the outskirts of their lives forever.

I will make contact at some point.

NADINE

Black ties. Ballgowns. And boring conversation. There are many perks to being a businessman's wife but having to attend events like this is not one of them.

I'm currently standing in the corner of this large function room and doing my best to stay out of the way of everybody else here as I sip from a champagne flute and watch my husband doing his thing. Max calls it networking, but we both know it is a little more cut-throat than that. He is doing his best to make as many contacts as he can in the hope that some of these wealthy people will be connected to the types of industries that he can sell his product to. My man looks friendly and charming and like he is simply here to make friends, but beneath that smooth veneer is a cold, calculating entrepreneur who is operating with one goal in mind.

Make more sales so his family can have a better life.

It's that fact that means I can't be too mad at him for making me attend things like this. I'd much rather be at home on the sofa wearing something a little more comfortable than a sparkly, sequinned dress, but needs must. It looks good for Max in the eyes of everyone else here if he turns up with a loyal woman on his arm, and it also helps me because I get to keep an eye on my man in a room full of several beautiful women.

Not everyone here has a ring on their finger and that fact, coupled with all the free booze that is flowing, means that things that shouldn't happen could easily do so if certain people weren't kept on a tight leash. That metaphorical leash could do with a little tug right now as I see a woman half my age saunter up to Max and start a conversation with him, so I make my way over and intricate myself into the exchange.

'I got you another champagne, dear,' I say as I hand Max the glass that I picked up from the waitress's tray as I walked across the busy room.

'Oh, thank you,' Max replies as he takes it, but the woman he was talking to also takes the hint that this is one man who is not on the menu tonight, and she leaves not long after I have made my presence known.

'So, how long do we have to stay?' I ask as I feel the bubbles going to my head.

'I told you not to come if you didn't fancy it.'

'I know, but it's not often you have one of these events so close to home. I thought it would be nice to spend a little more time together.'

'I appreciate that, but I'm working here, so I can't just leave early.'

'I didn't ask you to leave early. I just said-'

The sound of a spoon being hit against a glass interrupts all conversation in the room, and that's possibly a good thing because the start of the speeches seems to have prevented Max and me from getting into an argument.

The first speaker takes to the stage with a microphone in one hand and a glass of red wine in the other, and it becomes apparent he is very confident in front of an audience because he ends up waffling on for over twenty minutes. I zone out long before that, though,

31

and amuse myself by looking at my phone and seeing the latest social media posts from the kids.

Sophie has just posted an incredible photo from a beach in Thailand, and I make sure to like it, as well as leave a heart emoji underneath. Adam has also been busy, and while his day doesn't appear to have been as glamorous, it's still nice to see what he's been doing. The photo of him with his mates in his university's Student Union bar makes me smile, and I leave a comment saying, 'Have fun', even though I know he gets embarrassed by his mother commenting on his posts. But I'm not going to stop because as his mum, it's my duty to embarrass him from time to time, and now he's away at uni, this is the only way I can do that.

The second speech is only slightly more entertaining than the first. It's all about how it's not enough for the business leaders of today to show drive and initiative but that they have to start thinking outside the box when it comes to growing their company. That seems pretty obvious to me, but the business figures around me are lapping it up, and Max is one of them.

He was right. I shouldn't have come here. We're technically together, but he's not as present with me as I would like him to be.

I whisper in his ear that I need the bathroom, and then I walk away, snaking my way through the sea of stationary souls in black and white suits or flowing dresses before making it to the door that allows me to make my escape. The voice on the microphone is dulled out here, and that's a relief. One more minute of hearing somebody stating the obvious and I don't know what I would have done.

The bathroom at this venue is nowhere near as fancy as the ballroom, but I linger by the sinks and freshen up my make-up, pleased to see that I'm still looking good despite the champagne, the boredom and my advancing years.

My forties seemed to creep up on me. One minute I was turning heads as a twenty-something without any responsibilities in the world, the next, I was turning up to a surprise party where all my loved ones had gathered to help me celebrate reaching the beginning of 'midlife.'

Funny, but I didn't feel like celebrating it at the time.

Max seems to have adjusted to this new decade much better than I have, although I suppose the mansion, new sports car and ever-present need to grow his business beyond all realm of recognition could be signs that he is suffering from his own crisis as he begins to acknowledge his mortality. But what does this second chapter of life have in store for us? The first brought marriage, kids and a whole heap of fun. But what's next? Plucking out greys and reminiscing on the past?

Max really was right. I shouldn't have come here because now I've had too much champagne, and I'm getting all deep and thoughtful. I should have just made do with our Friday nights at the Italian. Forcing myself to be around my husband more is only going to lead to even more problems between us.

And so it proved.

I got progressively more drunk as the evening went on, as did Max, and by the time we were in the taxi home, we were bickering. He accused me of not making an effort with the other people at the event. I accused him of trying too hard and not being himself. Then I said he was neglecting me. He said I didn't understand what it took to run a business. I scoffed. He rolled his eyes. I wanted to hit him, not to hurt him but just to show that I felt we were heading towards a dangerous place if we didn't snap out of this. But I didn't. I left him untouched, just like he left me untouched when we got home and let the poor taxi driver be on his way.

This time it's my turn to sit up with a nightcap while Max has gone upstairs to pretend to be asleep when we both end up in bed. At least our Fridays at *San Bella* result in some good food. I barely got a chance to sample some of the canapes tonight before they ran out.

Sophie has posted another photo. She's been swimming in the sea, and it's beautiful, but it's another reminder of how far away she is from home. Adam has no further updates, but I notice he has deleted the comment I left under his photo earlier. That stings a little. But I know he loves me. Just like I know Max loves me. So what am I missing? Why do I have such a wonderful family yet feel so lonely?

It's easy to think that I'm the only person who feels this way but, of course, that won't be the case. The world is full of lonely souls. I bet there's someone else in this town who is experiencing the same emotions at this very moment. I wonder what coping mechanisms they use. Do they have actual tactics, or do they just stubbornly carry on and wait for things to get better?

I wish I could meet one of those people.

I could ask them.

Who knows? We might even become friends.

HANNAH

It's been a quiet week at the restaurant, and I blame it on the weather. Who wants to get dressed up and go out for a meal when the rain is horizontal and the winds are blowing a gale? While it's the job of the manager to worry about low reservations, I am still affected because fewer people dining and drinking means fewer people tipping. Then again, I know I'll never be rich, so there's no point crying over a few lost pound coins.

Thankfully, Friday is on the horizon again, and I'm already counting down the hours. I know that night will be busy because it always is, but most importantly, I know that night will see Mr and Mrs Murphy come back into my life for a couple of hours. Until then, I will keep myself occupied as I always do.

Outside of work, I don't do much, but one thing I always make sure to fit into my schedule at least twice a week is to visit the local graveyard. That's not because I'm morbid but because there are a couple of headstones belonging to people I used to know. I like to pay my respects regularly and today is another example of that.

I'm taking advantage of a brief lull in the rain to be out and about as I move along the path that cuts through this depressing but well-maintained resting place for the dead. I've brought flowers with me like all good mourners should, and the cheap but colourful bunch of lilies are definitely going to brighten up the graves in question. It took me a little while to find the headstones when I first came here, but once I had the route, I've been back again and again until it was ingrained in my mind. I almost feel like I could find my way with my eyes closed now, but I won't put that to the test. The last thing I want to do is trip over someone's headstone and find myself face down on a grave.

It would be hard to rest in peace with my weight crashing down on top of the poor soul under the soil.

I pass an elderly woman with tears in her eyes, and my heart breaks for the partner she has presumably lost. There's nothing better than falling in love, but there's nothing worse than losing that other person and trying to find a way to go on. It's possible. But it is not easy.

The woman shuffles away, and I wish I could stop and give her a hug. But I don't. She's done what she needs to do here, and now it's time for me to do the same.

'Guess who's back,' I say as I reach the two headstones that stand side by side, protruding out of the grass that has got a little long and could do with a trim. I presume the groundskeeper here is waiting for the earth to dry out a little before he gets the lawnmower out, but based on the weather forecast, I think he's going to be waiting a while. But in the meantime, I can do my bit to spruce up this area, and I place the flowers down by the headstone on the left.

It's the one that belongs to Michael Spinner, and along with his name, the headstone gives the years he was alive.

1985-2020.

Yes, this poor man died young, well before his time. But life isn't fair.

'Hi babe,' I say to Michael as if he can hear me and could offer up a response. But the only reply I do get comes in the sound of the wind rustling the leaves on the tall oak trees that surround this spooky place.

'It's been a tough week this week. Work's rubbish as usual. And this weather is getting me down. But I feel better for seeing you.'

The wind grows stronger, and I wait for it to settle before I speak again.

'I hope you're not cold. I can't imagine what it must be like to have to be out here all day. Then again, it's not exactly warm where I am. I still don't put the heating on. But I got a new hoody last week at the charity shop, and I wear it to bed sometimes. It keeps me cosy.'

I notice the old woman from earlier walking back the way she came just then, and I wonder what she could be doing. I keep watching her to find out, and it's not long until I see her pick up her handbag from beside one of the graves. She must have left it there by mistake. Forgetful, but at her age, she can be forgiven for that.

'I might forget some things as I get older, but I won't ever forget you,' I go on. 'You'll always be up here.' I tap the side of my head. 'And you know you will always be in here too.' I touch the centre of my chest.

The woman with the handbag looks at me as she walks away, and for a moment, I worry that she is going to come over and say something to me. Has she noticed which grave I am standing in front of? No, I guess not, because she just walks away. She's got enough of her own problems. Why concern herself with mine as well?

With the wind lowering my body temperature a little more with each passing second, I decide that I won't make this one of my longer visits. But I'm not done yet, and I turn my attention to the second headstone now. This one belongs to Victoria Spinner, and like the man she is buried beside, she too passed away in her mid-thirties. But unlike Michael, I won't be talking to this lost soul. Instead, I just glare at the name inscribed into the stone for long enough for whatever spirit resides beneath it to get the message.

The wind drops all of a sudden, casting an eerie silence over the graveyard, and as I glance up at the leaves, I see they are strangely still. It almost feels as if I am the only thing alive in this vicinity, and that gives me a sense of strength as if I'm stronger than I thought I was when I first arrived here a few minutes ago. But it doesn't take long for the wind to pick back up again, shaking the trees and reminding me that I'm not as powerful as I was enjoying thinking I was. Those trees were here before me, and they will surely be here after me. I'm just as vulnerable as all the people buried here. But it's not my time yet. I still have so much to live for.

I have one more important thing to say to Michael before I leave and go home to get ready for my next shift at *San Bella,* and it's something that I say to him every time I visit.

'I'm sorry.'

Of all the things I have said, that is the thing I want him to hear the most. But I don't know if it is possible. At least I've tried. That's all I can do. It's all any of us can do.

'I'll be back soon, babe. But you already know that.'

With that, I turn and leave, striding away before I linger for too long and end up with tears in my eyes like that old woman. But despite my urgency, my emotions still manage to get the better of me, and I'm pretty much crying by the time I reach the gates.

Damn it. I didn't bring a tissue with me today. That's because I had told myself that I wasn't going to get upset. It's been two years now. Two years and I'm still blubbering away. I need to get a grip. Pull myself together. One way to do that would be to stop coming here. But I'm not prepared to do that yet. That's because I haven't moved on. I can only do that if I find somebody else. But filling a hole in the heart is not easy. It takes a special kind of person to replace a lost soulmate.

Do I have anyone in mind?

I might do, but it's complicated.

Just like the story of how Mr and Mrs Spinner ended up in the ground.

NADINE

I've been sorting through some of Adam's things today in the loft. I'm not throwing anything away because I'll keep these items for memory's sake if he doesn't want them himself. But I'm just trying to get a little more organised, and it won't hurt to kill a couple of hours of my afternoon either.

Max is away in Leeds, pitching to another client, and he won't be back until tomorrow. He spends at least half his week in various hotel rooms in various cities, but he doesn't seem to mind it. I have told him to hire an actual salesman to do all the travelling for him, but he insists on doing it himself. "No one is as passionate about my product as I am" is what he always says, and I suppose he is right. I'm certainly not as passionate about it as him. Who can get excited about an air-conditioning filter? But Max can, and that's good because without that passion, he'd be earning a lot less.

Tackling another cardboard box full of items from my son's childhood, I pull out football trophies, school reports and even an old story he wrote once in his youth. Everything is mixed in together, but I'm trying to create a system now. One box for school things, another for hobbies. Not only will it create more space, but there will come a time when Max and I are no longer here, and I want my kids to have one less headache on their hands when it comes to going through our possessions.

But like all trips down memory lane, it's a journey fraught with emotion, and it doesn't take me long to stop being productive and end up just sitting with my legs crossed on the floor, reading through Adam's old school reports and recalling the bright little boy he used to be. He was always better at the more creative subjects like English and Art rather than Maths and Science, and that's evident in the grades on these report cards. There's a wild contrast between A's and D's, but overall, he was a good student, and all his teachers agreed he was no trouble.

Unlike his mother.

I was terrible at school, barely making the effort to turn up, never mind trying to pass exams. I can say that life turned out well, regardless of my attitude towards education, but looking back, I'm not proud of how I used to treat my teachers. Thankfully, neither of my kids took after me in that respect, and I didn't get anywhere near as much hassle as my parents got with me.

Being surrounded by Adam's things is only making me miss him even more now that he's moved out, and I think about giving him a call to see how he's getting on. But what if he doesn't answer because he's busy in a lecture or having too much fun with a new friend he's made? I don't want to hassle him. He'll call me when he wants to talk.

However, as I sit here in this dimly lit loft full of old things that came with us from the last house, I'm aware that it's not just a mother's love that is making me want to reach out to my son. It's guilt too, as well as a need to double-check and make sure my secret is still safe.

Adam is my son.

But he is not Max's.

I'm the only person that knows that fact in this family. My husband, my son and my daughter have no idea there is a terrible secret hanging over all of our heads that could blow this family apart if it ever came out. The only other person who knows the truth is Kieran, the man I had a brief fling with a year before Adam was born.

It was stupid. I knew it at the time, and I haven't changed my opinion on that in the nineteen years since. I could blame it on being young, but I wasn't that young. I was in my mid-twenties, so there's no excuse really. I was old enough to know what I was doing and that it was very, very wrong.

Cheating on Max was a bad call, but Kieran came into my life at a time when I was feeling a little overwhelmed with things. I was married to a hard-working, ambitious man who made me feel proud but also a little insignificant whenever I compared my talents to his. I was a mother to a young daughter who demanded so much of my time and energy that I could barely remember the person I used to be before breastfeeding and burping was a thing. And I was battling the doubts that were telling me I had settled down too soon, not helped by the knowledge that a few of my friends were off on adventures around the world while I was stuck at home sifting through a pile of bills and dirty nappies.

I was happy with my life at that time - I can see that now, but I was also feeling a little confused.

Enter Kieran.

I met him in the supermarket, of all places. Tinned goods aisle, if you must know. I was there alone after leaving Sophie with her grandparents. Such an act had given me the time to do all the other jobs I was struggling to fit in, like showering and shopping, and while visiting the supermarket was hardly a break, it was a brief moment of calm in an otherwise busy existence.

It was perhaps a consequence of my tired, bedraggled mind that had caused me to accidentally drop several tins of tomato soup all over the floor, and as they clattered across the aisle, a fellow shopper came to my aid. After scooping up some of the cans and chuckling at my apology, he told me that everything was okay and that none of the tins had cracked, meaning a mop and bucket was not going to be needed. Then he smiled at me, and I caught him glancing down at my left hand.

It was at that moment that I realised I had forgotten to put my wedding ring back on after my shower.

I always used to take it off before washing in those days because the fit wasn't quite right on it, and it often came loose when my hands were all soapy. Being terrified of losing the small diamond ring down the plughole, I had taken to removing it before stepping under the jets of water in my bathroom. But that day, I had forgotten to return it to my fourth finger, and it seemed that the good Samaritan in the supermarket had then assumed that I was single and therefore, prime for a pick-up attempt.

I could have told him that I was taken and brushed off his questions, thanking him for helping me before pushing my trolley away and carrying on with my errands. But I didn't. I stood and listened to him, and the more we chatted, the more I forgot about all the jobs on my to-do list and the more I realised it had been a long time since anybody had paid me this much attention. It didn't take Kieran long to start flirting, and while I wasn't overly encouraging him, I wasn't shutting him down either. Perhaps it was only inevitable that he then saw it fit to ask for my phone number.

But why did I have to give it to him?

I'd left the supermarket that day in a daze. It almost felt like it was all a dream, and I hadn't actually done what I had. Like one of those nightmares where you commit a terrible crime only to wake up and feel that overwhelming relief that it didn't actually happen. But this was no dream. It had happened. I was a married woman, and I had just swapped numbers with a guy who had been hitting on me.

It hadn't taken long for Kieran to send me a message, but it had taken a while before I had plucked up the courage to respond. At first, I was going to just delete the text, try and forget about it and hope to never bump into him in the supermarket again. But after a particularly bad night with Sophie, in which Max had been more of a hinderance than a help, I had found myself reaching for my phone in my sleep-deprived state and typing out a text of my own.

I agreed to meet him for a drink during the day, knowing I could leave my daughter with my parents again and also knowing that Max would be at work, so

45

he would be none the wiser. But just before meeting Kieran, I did something else.

I took off my wedding ring again.

Adam's school reports are starting to weigh heavier in my hands as I remain sitting on the loft floor whilst thinking back over the sins of my past. But it's nothing compared to the weight of carrying this secret around with me for almost half of my life.

After meeting Kieran for a drink, he played the gentleman and didn't want to take things too quickly. But I was the opposite. I felt like I had to rush because I feared I was going to get caught at any second, and that was why I suggested we go back to his place. I don't think there are too many single men around who would have refused an idea like that, and Kieran was certainly not one of them. We ended up at his that fateful afternoon, and by the time I left, I had not only cheated on Max emotionally, but physically too.

I ended up seeing Kieran three more times after that before I came to my senses and called it quits. I confessed to him that I was married, and I had experienced a moment of madness, or rather, several moments of madness as he rightly pointed out. But he accepted it when I told him I wished for our fling to remain a secret, and then I walked away, expecting, or rather hoping, that I would never see him again.

Then I missed my period.

I locked myself in the bathroom and cried as I wished it wasn't so, but I was pregnant again, and I knew that my husband was not the father. It took me a while to realise that I could continue with the pregnancy, and Max wouldn't be any the wiser. I just kept my pregnancy status quiet, seduced my husband as soon as I could, and then told him that I had returned a positive test not long after that.

He believed the baby was his. So I kept it. Adam arrived. And out of a terrible mistake, something truly wonderful had happened. I had a son to go with my daughter, and it seemed like I had gotten away with it.

Until Kieran came back into my life.

I'd changed supermarkets out of fear of seeing him again, but I couldn't do much about bumping into him on the high street one sunny Tuesday afternoon. I had been pushing Adam in his stroller when I saw him coming towards me, and despite trying to change course and duck into the nearest shop, Kieran caught up with me. It was impossible for him not to notice Adam, just like it was impossible to not see the resemblance between father and child. Despite that, I pretended like he wasn't his, but he was never stupid, and after figuring out the dates could match, he asked me outright.

Was Adam his?

I'd almost collapsed at that moment, fearing like my life was going to crash down all around me, and it was as if I wanted to get a head start on it by falling over myself. But my weak reaction to the question gave Kieran the answer he was seeking. He knew he was the father. All I needed to know then was what he planned on doing with that information.

To my eternal relief, Kieran panicked and said he was starting a job abroad soon and couldn't deal with this. I sensed an opportunity and quickly told him that it was not his problem if he didn't want it to be. He could just leave. Get on that plane. Pretend like this never happened. It was for my sake as much as his, but he agreed to it. He apologised and asked would I be okay? I told him I was. He knew this was a secret I was desperate to keep quiet.

And so he left.

I've not seen Kieran since that day, and I hope I won't see him until the day I die. I don't know what became of Adam's real father, but I do know what became of the boy we created. He grew into a fine young man who believes he has two perfect parents. Me. And Max. It's not the truth, but I will do anything to stop him from becoming damaged. And I will do anything to keep Max from knowing what I did behind his back.

I'm not a bad person.

I feel like I have atoned for my sins through almost two decades of guilt weighing on my conscience.

But I can't look at any more of Adam's things today, so I leave the loft quickly and go back downstairs where I won't be reminded of the past quite so easily.

It's just a secret, and we all have them.

Don't we?

HANNAH

We've had a complaint from one of the customers. It's from a well-dressed but bolshy man on Table Eight. He is part of a five-strong party of similarly dressed and similarly bolshy men who came in at seven o'clock after what I can only suspect was a boozy afternoon elsewhere. I guess the weekend started early for those guys, but I'm not having quite as much fun as they are today.

The man said his steak wasn't cooked correctly. He wanted it medium-rare. He apparently got it medium-well. Now he has returned his food to the kitchen, and if there is one thing that gets a chef angry, it is seeing food come back. To make matters worse, the man in question is on one of my tables, so I'm the poor person who now has to act as the messenger between the unhappy patron and the unhappy chef.

'He's asked if you can cook him another one, Chef,' I try, but I doubt that will elicit a good response from my colleague on the other side of the hot counter.

'Where's the docket?' Chef Williams demands to know, and he grabs the pile of papers that are skewered on a spike. These represent all the meals that have already been cooked, but they are also a good way of determining who is in the right. Did the chef mess up the order? Unlikely. Did the customer change his mind? Most probably. Or did I just get the order wrong when I placed it? *Hopefully not.*

To my relief, it seems it is a rare mistake on the part of the chef and while he doesn't apologise, he does

49

start cooking another steak, telling me to wait because it will be ready very soon.

I'd much rather step out of this steaming kitchen, but I do as I'm told because that's how it works in restaurants. There's a clear pecking order, and waitresses are way below the people who cook the food we serve.

But there's another reason for me wanting to get out of the kitchen other than needing to cool down. It's because I know the Murphys are out there.

As it's Friday, they are seated as usual at Table Six. And as always, I am not tasked with serving them, but that doesn't mean I can't eavesdrop on a few things they say whenever I pass their table with a pile of plates.

So far this evening, I have heard Mr Murphy mention something about the hotel in Leeds not being up to standard, while I heard Mrs Murphy say that she was making progress sorting through the items in the loft. Okay, so it's hardly the kind of soundbites that give me a full picture of the lives they lead outside of this restaurant, but it's something to keep me entertained during my shift.

The steak is ready as quickly as the chef promised it would be, and he urges me to leave the kitchen quickly. I'm only too happy to do so, and while I don't get much in the way of a thank you from the man who ordered the slab of red meat a while ago now, at least it's one problem taken care of. But there's another problem waiting for me only a second later.

'So, how long have you worked here for?'

The question has been asked of me by the solitary man at Table Twelve. He's the same guy I saw in here last Friday night and just like that first time, he is eating alone. While I had originally felt a little sorry for him earlier in the night and made as much small talk as I could, I'm now starting to regret being so pleasant because I think he might have misinterpreted my friendliness for something more.

I don't really have the time to stand around and answer questions about myself on the busiest night of the week at this restaurant, but I also can't ignore the customers or I might get a complaint against me. I'll just have to answer quickly and then get back to work.

'Too long,' I say with a smile, hoping a little humour will be enough to satisfy his curiosity. But it's not and he presses me for a better answer before I can walk away.

'Seriously, I'm interested. How long have you worked here for?'

'A few years.'

'You like it here?'

'Erm, it's okay, I guess.'

'You must like it if you have stayed for so long.'

'I suppose.'

'Unless there's something else you would rather be doing. Is there?'

'Not really.'

'You haven't got any other dreams or ambitions besides being a waitress?'

I frown because this is getting very deep, and I'm not used to these kind of conversations with

51

anybody, never mind one of the people I serve at *San Bella*. But the man must take my frown as a sign that he has possibly offended me because he apologises.

'I'm sorry. I didn't mean to say that being a waitress is not a worthy profession. It's a very important one, and I for one, am glad that you are here to serve me.'

'That's okay. I'm not offended. But I do need to check on a few of the other tables. Unless there's something I can get you?'

'No, I'm okay for now. Thank you.'

I smile at the man and then walk away quickly before he can say anything else. That was weird but otherwise, harmless. I guess he just wants someone to talk to. Maybe he should invite a friend to dinner next time, so he isn't by himself. Unless he doesn't have a friend. I hope that's not the case. Not only would that be sad, but it would most likely mean he will keep bothering me every time he comes here.

'Excuse me?'

I freeze beside the table to my left but only because I know which one it is.

It's Table Six. The Murphys. Mr Murphy has just stopped me.

What does he want?

'Er, yes? Is everything okay?' I ask him, surprising myself by how nervous I feel as I stand so close to him and his wife.

He looks even more handsome up close than he does from across the room, whilst I can really get a better idea of just how much makeup his wife is wearing now I'm standing over her.

'We ordered another bottle of red wine with our waitress twenty minutes ago, but we don't seem to have had it yet,' Mr Murphy tells me and he's not angry, just disappointed, which somehow seems worse.

'Oh, I'm so sorry about that. I'll check on it for you now.'

'Thank you.'

Mr Murphy returns to his meal, and I scurry away to the kitchen to look for the waitress who has neglected his drinks order. It doesn't take me too long to find her.

'Becki, did Table Six ask you for another bottle of red wine?'

Becki frowns as if I've just asked her to try and remember something from a history class and not something that happened twenty minutes ago. Then she shrugs and says she doesn't think so. But I'm not willing to take that as an answer because in a choice between choosing who to believe between a respectable man having dinner with his wife and a bored teenager who couldn't care less about anybody other than herself, I think I know who is in the right here.

'Table Six is your table. They asked you for another bottle of wine. You need to go and get it for them and apologise for the delay.'

'Calm down, Mum,' Becki says as she rolls her eyes, and that last word gets a snigger from one of the other irritating youngsters that I have to work with.

'Why are you calling me that?'

'I don't know. Because it's funny.'

'But I'm not your mum.'

'You sound like her. And you're the same age as her. Although she has better hair.'

I would love nothing more than to push Becki's beautiful but bitchy face towards one of the hot pans sizzling away only a few feet from where we stand in this kitchen, but that won't do any good. She might lose her looks and her rotten attitude, but I would lose my job and with that, my chance to be near the Murphys every Friday night. It also won't get Mr Murphy his bottle of wine any quicker. That's why I take a deep breath and compose myself before speaking again.

'You need to look after them,' I say quietly but forcefully.

'Why?'

'Because they are your responsibility.'

'Yeah, they're mine. Not yours. So why do you care?'

'Do you want to lose your job?'

'Do you think I'm bothered about that?'

'Maybe not. But it's not fair on everyone else who works here if you give us a bad reputation.'

'Oh, get a life.'

'No, you get a life! Now go and get that bottle of wine for Mr Murphy!'

'Or what?'

'Just do it!'

Becki seems shocked by my outburst, but she's not the only one. I've surprised myself by how worked up I've got. But at least it has done the trick. Becki leaves to go and do what she should have done twenty minutes ago, and I'm relieved that the Murphys won't be waiting any longer than they have to for their next drink.

But despite most of the insolent nonsense my colleague just spouted, there was something in all of it that was correct.

Why do I care?

I don't know. Perhaps they remind me of another couple I used to know.

I do care about the Murphys. I'm fascinated by them. And now that I have had a little taste of being nearer to them, I want more.

NADINE

Television shows can make some people's lives look so glamorous. I don't know who the bigger fool is. The person who believes everything they see on reality TV or the person who knows it's all nonsense but still watches it anyway. I would fall into that latter category of audience member because I've spent all morning watching episodes of such a show.

Housewives of Australia is the name of it, and while I could try and pretend that I put it on to inject a little Aussie sunshine into my life with sights of Bondi Beach and beyond, I would be lying. I've been watching it because it's entertaining, and it also reminds me of the time I almost participated in a show just like it.

Perhaps it was my own version of a mid-life crisis that had seen me apply for a spot on *Housewives at Home*, a UK reality show in which the camera was to follow the lives of eight women who were married to successful businessmen and who had a penchant for some of the finer things in life. It seemed like a fun idea at the time, particularly after a bottle of wine, but I had not expected to make the shortlist.

So imagine my surprise when I found out that I had been called for an audition.

I was a bundle of nerves on the day I journeyed to the TV studio, but I relaxed a little when I saw how many other women had been called too. It seemed like the producers hadn't been particularly selective in who they had summoned to audition, and that made me realise I was probably not going to get much further.

With the nerves having dissipated, I was able to be my usual, confident self in the audition when the cameras were trained on me, and that must have been why I was selected to go to the next round.

And the next. And the next.

Suddenly, before I knew it, I was one round away from being chosen to be the next big reality star.

Forget about the reality of the glamorous world of television. It was more the reality of my face being all over TV screens in the UK that caused me to come to my senses at the last minute and withdraw from the process. I'd like to say I did that because I decided that I didn't need the fame or adulation because I realised I was already enough without it. But it wasn't because of that. Rather, I pulled out because I had realised that Kieran could see me on TV, hear me talking about my son, Adam, and suddenly decide that he wanted to make contact again.

I have no way of ever knowing if that would have been the case, but I didn't tempt fate, and that was why I never became the reality star I was possibly destined to be. The eight women who did get selected were all fairly famous for the two years the show ended up running for, and it did look like a lot of fun from what I saw when I tuned in to a couple of the episodes. But I know I made the right decision. I maintained a low profile and kept my name and face out of the limelight, and because of that, there was no risk of Kieran having second thoughts about what he said to me all those years ago.

Skipping the show also meant I avoided being trolled online by all the cretins who use social media to try and bring down those in the public eye, so that was another bonus. I'm not sure how well I would have handled having millions of people commenting on my appearance, my lifestyle and my opinions on everything from politics to my favourite holiday destination. As it is, I can keep all those things to myself as I lie here on the sofa and watch other people parading themselves around for a paycheque.

But there's only so much reality TV I can watch before I start to feel guilty about wasting my day, so it doesn't take me long to get my shoes and coat on and get out of the house to go and do a bit of shopping in town. The weather is clear, unlike my cluttered mind, but there's nothing like a little retail therapy to perk me up. Two hours later and with several shopping bags hanging from my arms, I'm feeling much better about things.

I'll never forget how I have lied to my husband and my son, but I can have a few brief moments of respite in the long day.

It's a relief to make it back to my car and unload all the shopping bags onto the back seat, and the plan now is to go home and hang these items in my wardrobe before Max can see how much I bought. But just before I start the engine, I check my phone, and that's when I notice I have several missed calls from Adam.

It seems he's suddenly decided to stop ignoring me and now needs me urgently. But why? My first guess is that he has run out of money, having overspent in the student bars, and needs a top-up in his bank account.

Either that or he has had an attack of conscience and realised he should probably check in with his dear mother at least once during his first term. But I'm not foolish enough to think it's the latter, so I already have my mind set on transferring him some extra spending money as I call him back and wait for him to answer.

When he does pick up, he sounds annoyed and definitely not like somebody who is about to ask a favour.

'Why didn't you answer your phone?'

'I'm sorry, love. I've been shopping, and I didn't hear it in my handbag. What's wrong?'

I'm waiting for him to say the word 'money', but instead, he says a word I never wanted to hear him say.

'Who's Kieran?'

The phone almost falls from my hand as I try to breathe properly and convince myself my world isn't seconds away from imploding.

'What?'

'Who's Kieran?'

'What are you talking about?'

Please tell me there is a perfectly reasonable explanation for why my son is using this man's name. Or just any reason that won't result in Adam telling me he never wants to see me again.

'I got a letter from somebody called Kieran, and they told me they were one of your old friends.'

'A letter. What letter?'

'It just came to my student halls.'

Has Kieran been following Adam?

'What did it say?'

'Not much. It was weird. The guy just said he was a friend of yours and wanted to reach out to wish me well at university. Who is it?'

'I don't know. Did he say anything else?'

'He said that he wanted to make contact with me sooner but had not been sure if it was the right thing to do.'

Shit. It sounds like Kieran has changed his mind about not wanting to be a dad. Then again, it has been nineteen years. I imagine he has grown up a lot in that time, just like our son has.

'What else did he say?'

'Nothing. He just left a phone number and said I could call him if I wanted to talk.'

I feel like I could be sick, but I have to hold myself together long enough to make sure this isn't going to get any worse.

'Did you call it?' I ask as the fear rises up in my throat.

'No, I almost did, but I thought it was a bit strange, so I wanted to check with you.'

'That's good. Don't call it.'

'Who is this guy?'

'Nobody. It doesn't matter.'

'Why has he written to me? How does he know where I am?'

'I don't know, but it's nothing to worry about. But I want you to come home. Can you do that?'

'What? No, it's halfway through term.'

'I need you to come home right away.'

'Why?'

'Because I need to tell you something, and I don't want to do it over the phone.'

I realise then that I could go to him. It would certainly be much quicker than waiting for my son to summon up the energy to catch a train.

'I can be with you in a couple of hours,' I say as I mentally run through the route to his campus in my head. I've only been there twice before, once on the open day and once when we left him on his first day. Max did the driving both times, but I'm sure I can find the way with a Sat-Nav.

'Why don't you just tell me on the phone? I've got stuff to do here.'

'I need to see you. I won't be long. I'll call you when I'm on campus.'

'Why are you being weird?'

'Just wait for me to get there, okay? I love you. See you soon.'

With that, I hang up and put the car in motion, speeding out of the shopping centre car park like an F1 driver on a final qualifying lap. It's Friday, which means I should be going to *San Bella* with Max tonight, but that is not going to happen now. This is far more important.

Why has this happened? How has Kieran found Adam? And what does he want with him now that he has?

If there's someone in this town with a bigger problem than me right now then I'd like to meet them because I find it hard to believe that there is.

HANNAH

It's another late-night portion of cheesy chips to round off my Friday evening. But they taste different this week. Too much salt. Or not enough. Maybe they changed the type of cheese they use. No, that's not it either. I know what it is, and it's got nothing to do with the quality of the food. Rather, it's got everything to do with the person consuming it.

I'm confused, distracted, worried. I'm that way because this was the first Friday night without the Murphys coming into the restaurant. I checked the reservation book as I always did and saw their name listed beside the time and table. But they didn't show up. Table Six sat empty for a while before it was eventually assigned to another couple who had made it to *San Bella*.

I felt frustrated to see somebody else sitting in the seats that should have been occupied by Mr and Mrs Murphy, but there wasn't much I could do about it. All I could do was wonder what might have caused my new favourite couple to deviate from their routine.

Was one of them ill? Or had there been an accident? Those two options are troubling for me, but there is another option that makes me feel even worse.

It's the possibility that they have found something else to do with their Friday night.

The thought of never seeing either of them again makes me feel sick. That feeling then reminds me how empty my life is. How can I be this invested in a couple who I don't even know? They don't even know me either. We're literally strangers, yet I find myself missing them when they're not around me.

This is just what I do. I get attached to things. To people. To ideas. The idea that I could be happy and have what the Murphys have. But that's all it will ever be. An idea.

Unless I act on it.

Throwing the remains of the chips into the black bin bag on the kitchen floor, I wonder if I should have taken Mario up on his latest offer for us to hang out after he had finished his shift in the takeaway. I could have invited him back here, and that would mean I wouldn't be alone again now.

The house is cold and empty, and I'm missing my boyfriend again. But I'm not ready to go to bed yet and sleep off this latest bout of loneliness. Instead, I find myself wandering around our home in the darkness, running my fingers along the surfaces in each room.

One way to describe this place would be to say it was minimalist. Only the absolute essentials are here. We don't like clutter. It makes it hard to think. I always say that my mind is cluttered enough, so I need my surroundings to be as clear and clean as possible. It makes it easier to think. No mess. No distraction. Just enough.

An outsider might say that this home is lacking in character and, in turn, warmth. But it has to be like this. It simply wouldn't work any other way.

I'm in the bathroom now, staring at my reflection in the mirror and noticing how ghastly pale I am. If anyone could do with a suntan, then it's me. But there's not much chance of getting one of those in this town at this time of the year. Hopefully, we'll go on holiday soon. Me and my man. Somewhere warm and exotic. I hear Mexico is the place to be these days. Then again, all the girls at work seemed to be obsessed with Dubai.

I hear them all chattering to each other on our breaks. They talk about such and such an influencer and how much she is getting paid to post poolside photos from under the palm trees in that desert city. They talk as if such a thing is possible in their futures and that they won't be waitresses forever. I'm not sure they will ever get to the point where they get paid to upload selfies from sunny climes, but I am fairly confident none of them will be working at *San Bella* for much longer. Why would they? They are young, and they are full of dreams and aspirations. More importantly, they still have the energy required to try and go after them.

One of the waitresses left a couple of months ago. Rebekah. Stormed out halfway through her shift. Said life was too short for this shit, or something to that effect. I didn't witness the last few moments of her time at *San Bella,* but from what I heard, it was quite entertaining.

It was a shame because I actually liked her. Unlike the others, she had a bit of personality. Or perhaps I liked her because she was the only one who was nice to me. She would say hello and goodbye, and while that doesn't sound like much, it's a damn sight more respect than I'm used to getting from people.

But there was more to it than that. Rebekah and I had a couple of interesting conversations whenever we were on shift together. Nothing too deep. Just about what we would do if we weren't serving hungry customers in an Italian. I said I'd be travelling the world but only because I suspected that was the kind of answer she wanted to hear. I could hardly be honest with her and say that I was actually quite happy working in the restaurant and that I believed life was more about the people in it rather than the activities one got up to.

But that is the truth. I don't care about skydiving in The Seychelles or backpacking around Berlin. Not really. I just want love and the comforting knowledge that comes with knowing I am enough, not just for someone else, but for me too. But I gave the less complex answer, and Rebekah lapped it up before telling me that she wanted to travel too. It was funny, though. She never suggested we should travel together. Why would she? I was almost old enough to be her mum. It was silly of me to ever think we were friends, which of course, we weren't. A friend wouldn't walk out without saying goodbye.

But I do miss her. She was a bit of a thinker in a world where I feel that most people let others do the thinking for them. I guess that's why she decided she was wasting her youth and walked out so abruptly. I envy her for that. Making a decision and then just seeing it through. Who knows whether it will work out better in the end, but at least she has tried. I used to be like her, but I've become hesitant these days. That might be because of what happened the last time I took a risk and put myself out there, but it could also be because I'm now letting fear control me.

I wish I knew what happened to the Murphys tonight. It's driving me mad not knowing. I wish I'd followed them home one Friday night. That way, I would know their address, and I could at least go and check on the house now. I might catch a glimpse of them through the windows, and then I would know they were alright. They wouldn't ever have to know I was there. I could go unseen. Like a guardian angel watching over somebody, protecting but not looking for any attention or recognition. If I ever see them again, then I will make sure I have a backup plan to keep them in my life under my terms.

It's late now. 2 am. I should call it a night. No point waiting up. Pulling my duvet over myself, I can smell the chips in the rubbish bag downstairs. I should probably take it out now, but I'll do it in the morning. It won't make any difference. I used to spend a lot of time worrying about doing something here that could get me in trouble. Leaving something out of place so that it was noticeable. Using too much energy and causing the bills to rise. Or cooking something that filled the home with a smell that required the windows to be left open for hours. But I've become a little less paranoid about all of that these days. I'm still careful, but I've figured out what works and where the limits are.

I don't want to upset anybody.

And I don't want to bring any extra attention upon me.

But I can't live like this forever. Something has to give eventually. And when it does, I just hope it's not as bad as last time.

NADINE

It had gone dark by the time I had made it onto campus at Adam's university. That lack of light contributed to my confusion as I struggled to find his halls, wandering around and growing frustrated because he wasn't picking up his phone and so couldn't guide me. But I eventually got my bearings and found the building we had dropped him off outside of on his first day as a student.

It had been a sunny September day when Max and I had driven Adam here to begin his first adventure away from home. The car had been full of bags, but my eyes had also been full of tears as I tried to comprehend not having my youngest child around the house anymore. We didn't stay long once we got him to his halls, mainly because Adam wanted us to make ourselves scarce in case we ruined his 'street cred' in front of his potential new mates. But I had made sure to get a quick hug in with him before we departed, knowing that was going to have to be enough to last me until the end of that first term.

That was the last time I had seen him, and I had expected that the next time would be under much better circumstances. Him coming home for the holidays and excitedly telling me all about what he had gotten up to while he had been away. The parties. The new friends. And hopefully, he had learnt a thing or two from his lecturers as well, although that might have been asking a little much from a 'Fresher'. Instead, I've seen him much sooner than anticipated but under circumstances I never would have wished for.

I could tell that Adam had already consumed some alcohol when he opened the door to his halls and walked out to meet me. He was a little fidgety and wide-eyed, although I also realised that could be down to him feeling awkward that his mother had just turned up to see him on a Friday night. The sounds of a nearby party had drifted out from an open kitchen window behind him, and I figured that was where he had just come from, but before he could go back there, we had something important to discuss.

'I still don't get why you had to drive all the way up here,' my son had said as he had led me to the side of the building to where I presumed he knew we would be out of the line of sight of the other students around here.

'Have you got the letter?'

'Yeah.'

'Give it to me.'

Adam had produced the piece of paper from his pocket then and handed it over, allowing me to get a good look at exactly what Kieran had written to our son.

Hello Adam,

My name is Kieran, and I am an old friend of your mother's. I wanted to reach out to you sooner, but I wasn't sure if it was the right thing to do. I want to wish you well with your studies at university. It must be a very exciting time for you, and I am sure you are going to have a lot of fun.

As I said, I wanted to get in touch sooner, but I was unsure. Perhaps it is best if you reach out to me next time, if you want to, of course.

My phone number is 07812 99235. Feel free to give me a call if you would like to talk at any time.

All the best.

I suppose I should have been grateful that Kieran hadn't signed off his letter 'From Dad'. But even though he spared me that disaster, the content of the note made it clear that he now wanted to play a much bigger role in the life of his long-lost son.

'So who the hell is this guy?' Adam had asked me as I had been reading the letter for a second time. 'I almost called him when you were driving up here, just to get some answers.'

'You never call this number! Do you hear me?'

'Why not?'

'Because this man is dangerous.'

Adam had been shocked at my answer, but I had held it together as the words had come out of my mouth, mainly because it had been the course of action I had decided to take during my drive to campus. I had settled on the idea of telling Adam that Kieran was an old boyfriend, someone who I knew before I met Max, and that he had not taken it well when I had broken up with him. He had never hurt me, I assured Adam of that, but he had displayed some troubling tendencies over the years. In other words, he was a bit obsessed with me and my family.

'He's stalking you?' Adam had asked, looking stunned that anybody would find me interesting enough to be so fixated with.

'I wouldn't say stalking.'

'Then what? Do we need to go to the police?'

'No, definitely not!'

'What if this guy turns up looking for me? Would he hurt me?'

'No, of course not. I will handle this. You have nothing to worry about.'

I didn't have any confidence when I told my son that Kieran was not going to turn up, but I was at least confident that he wouldn't hurt him. He's Adam's dad. He just wants to get to know him. But I can't let that happen. And armed with the letter with Kieran's phone number on it, I at least had a way of getting in touch with the man from my past and telling him to stay away.

I had told Adam to let me know if anything else happened, but other than that, he was free to go back inside and re-join the party. He was happy enough with that, but just before he left, I had needed to give him one more instruction.

'Don't mention this to your father. I don't want him to know one of my exes is being weird.'

Thankfully, Adam could see why it would make sense to not bring Max in on these developments, and he had agreed to keep the letter between us. Then we said our goodbyes, and I was back on the road again, heading for home to salvage what was left of my Friday evening with my husband.

Max was disappointed when I told him that we would have to cancel our usual date night at *San Bella*, but I had told him we would get a takeaway when I got back. He bought my story about needing to visit Adam to drop off an emergency food parcel, and now he is waiting in the house, no doubt hungrily perusing the menu for the local Chinese and wishing I would walk through the door so he could order.

But I've not gone inside yet. I'm sitting in my car on the driveway, and I have one more thing to do before I go into our home.

I have to call the number in the letter.

I have to speak to Kieran.

For a man who is supposedly desperate to receive a call from his son, it takes Kieran a while to answer. But I get him on the line in the end, and when I hear him say hello, his voice transports me back in time.

'What the hell do you think you're doing sending a letter to Adam? And how did you find him? Have you been following him?'

I barely gave Kieran time to answer before I launched my next diatribe.

'You stay away from us. You hear me? You made your choice nineteen years ago. You said you couldn't deal with it. You moved abroad. That was your decision. You can't change your mind now. It's not fair on Adam. You'll destroy his childhood. He'll think it was all a lie.'

'It was a lie.'

'We agreed to keep it a secret!'

'I know, but that was then. I'm older now, and I've realised I've made mistakes. I want to atone for them. I want to get to know my son.'

'You can't do this!'

'Adam has a right to know. If he doesn't want to see me, then I will have to accept it. But he has to know I exist. You must see that?'

'All I see is someone being selfish and only thinking of himself. You'll ruin him if you keep this up, and you'll ruin me too. Is that what you want?'

'Do you have any idea what it's like to not be with your child?'

'No, because I've raised my children. You panicked and ran. It's no good having a guilty conscience over it now.'

'I don't know what you want me to do. You can't expect me to stop.'

'Please. I'm begging you. Leave us alone. Or…'

'Or what?'

'Or I'll go to the police. I'll say you've been stalking me. You must have been stalking Adam to send him the letter. How else did you know where he was?'

'I found his social media pages. All his profiles are public.'

Damn Zuckerberg and all the other website creators. Have they any idea how much trouble they have caused with their inventions?

'So you've been cyber-stalking him?'

'Now you're being ridiculous.'

'Am I? I'm just trying to protect my family. All you're doing is threatening it.'

'I don't know what you want me to say. But I can't walk away from this. If Adam doesn't reach out, then I will contact him again, and I'll tell him exactly who I am. I have a feeling he will call me then.'

I realise then that this isn't working, and I need to change tactics. What do they say? Keep your friends close and your enemies closer? I need to meet Kieran. Maybe that way, I can talk some sense into him.

'We need to talk. Properly. Can we meet next week? Wherever you want. So we can talk this over and come to some sort of arrangement.'

'I'm happy to meet you, but I'm not sure what you expect me to say.'

'We'll discuss that next week. I'll text you. In the meantime, stay away from Adam.'

Kieran assures me that he will, and we leave it at that.

It's probably no surprise that I'm not in the mood for a takeaway when I go inside and see Max, but he's starving, so I order enough to seem normal and force myself to eat a bit of it. But I don't sleep a wink all night.

It's been a hell of a day.

And it seems like there are even tougher days ahead.

But amazingly, I didn't even know the half of it.

HANNAH

I'm in awe of the women who just seem to look good without making much of an effort. I'm certainly not one of them. I'm looking decidedly average this evening, owing to my lack of make-up and the fact I haven't washed my hair today like I promised myself I would. But so what? It's a rare Monday at work for me, and the restaurant is quiet. I always slack off at the start of the week. It's only when it starts getting closer to Friday that I begin to step my game up and try to make myself look more presentable.

Another good thing about Mondays is not having to work with as many of the irritating waitresses as I do at the weekend. The early part of the week is like the graveyard shift in the hospitality industry, and those slots often go to the full-time staff, rather than the students or those who just need a little bit of cash on the busy nights. That means no Becki, Chrissy, or Tory. Just plain old Hannah tasked with looking after the only four tables of customers who are in this evening.

Or should that be five now?

I freeze as I stand on the edges of the restaurant floor and look towards the table by the window. It's the table that was unoccupied a few moments ago when I went into the kitchen. It's Table Six. The one the Murphys use at the same time every week.

But they are here now.

What?

It's not Friday. They shouldn't be here. I'm thrilled to see them, but I'm also terrified because I'm

75

the only waitress on duty, and that means I'll have to serve them. Oh, curse my bad luck. Why didn't I make more of an effort with my appearance? Instead of getting the prim and proper Becki with her long eyelashes and her fake tan, they're going to get a frumpy, greasy, make-up free me.

Damn it. What should I do?

Have I got time to try and spruce myself up? There might be a stick of lipstick somewhere in the changing rooms. Or perhaps there might be-

'Hannah. Can you take the drinks order for Table Six, please?'

The instruction from Francesco snaps me out of my trance and sends me scurrying over to the couple by the window. My heart is racing, and my hands are clammy, but whatever I do, I just need to make sure I don't mess their service up tonight. I can't think of anything worse than getting a complaint from the Murphys. I need them to like me.

That's the only way we can get closer.

'Good evening. Welcome to *San Bella*. Are you ready to order your drinks?'

I'm grinning like a Cheshire Cat and hoping that my overly pleasant demeanour will distract from my severely unkempt hair.

Mr Murphy looks up from his menu, and I can't tell if the confusion on his face is because I'm not his usual waitress or because he just hasn't decided what he wants to drink yet.

'Erm, what do you think, dear? Do you fancy wine this evening, or shall we just get soft drinks?'

I wonder if the husband's question to his wife is just him being a gentleman or because he's unsure what the sensible code of conduct is for drinking alcohol so early in the week. But it seems Mrs Murphy has no such qualms about any of it.

'Yes, I want wine.'

That was a very short and snappy answer, and I see Mr Murphy raise his eyebrows a little bit before he confers with the menu to try and find something that will satisfy his partner's thirst.

But the longer it takes for him to make a decision, the more I sense an opportunity.

'May I recommend the Malbec?' I say, trying to keep my voice calm and steady, even though I'm feeling almost as nervous as I did during my first ever shift here.

'Oh, okay,' he says. 'I'm happy to go with that one if you are, darling?'

'Yeah, fine. Whatever.'

Is Mrs Murphy always this rude? Or is she just having a bad day? I wonder what could have happened to cause them to deviate from their established routine. Then before I can stop the words, I'm already asking the question that reveals my curiosity.

'You guys usually come here on a Friday, don't you?' I say before instantly regretting it.

But it's out there now.

It's obvious how much I have been watching them.

'That's right,' Mr Murphy says with a smile that sets me at ease a little. 'We always sit at this same table. I guess it's hard not to notice us.'

I laugh a little too loudly for this quiet restaurant, and a few people look in my direction. But it's Mrs Murphy who I notice the most because she has looked up from her menu now, and she doesn't look particularly happy about me guffawing at her husband's mild joke.

'I think you usually get served by Becki,' I say, and I'm ready to walk away then because I don't want the woman at the table to get irritated with me. But before I can go, Mr Murphy speaks again.

'That's right. She's a good waitress, but she can be a little forgetful. I think it was you who helped us get our drinks quicker last time we came here.'

He's right, and I can't believe that he remembers that. The big grin on my face is almost impossible to tone down, but I manage it when I see Mrs Murphy still glaring at me.

'How about that bottle of wine?' she asks as a way of reminding me that I'm simply here to serve them with food and drink, not small talk.

'Of course. I'll be right back.'

I rush towards the bar without wasting another second and quickly tell my colleague behind it to get me a bottle of Malbec, pronto. But while he's searching the wine rack for the right thing, I glance back towards Table Six, and I feel a mixture of emotions.

On the one hand, I'm super excited that Mr Murphy remembers me. On the other, I'm sad that Mrs Murphy clearly doesn't care who I am and couldn't get rid of me quickly enough. I like him even more now than when I watched him from a distance. But I have to say that she has done very little to endear herself to me so far tonight.

With the bottle found and opened, I carry it back to the table by the window and offer to pour each of the diners a small sample to make sure that it is to their tastes. But Mrs Murphy tells me not to bother with any of that, and she just gestures for me to give her the bottle without wasting any more time.

I stand by rather uselessly as she pours her own glass first and gulps some of it down before even thinking about giving the bottle to her husband to share. He looks as surprised as I am, but I can't stand here all night, as much as I would like to. Annoyingly, I have other tables to serve, and I can see some of the people sitting at them are ready for the next stage of their meal. I wish it was just me and Table Six. That way, I could give them the personalised service they deserve instead of it being diluted by all the other people in here.

'I'll be back shortly to take your food order,' I tell the couple.

'Thank you, Hannah,' Mr Murphy says, noting my name badge, and just hearing him use my name sends a jolt of energy through me that I haven't felt in a long time.

'You're very welcome.'

I'm still smiling as I clear away the plates from Table Two and take the dessert order from Table Eight. In fact, it's a miracle I can even remember what cakes and cheeses they asked for because all I can think about is that man by the window. That polite, handsome man who remembers me. As for the woman he is sitting with, she is already on her second glass of wine. She's either thirsty or stressed or both. But then it occurs to me that they no longer have to be a mystery. Now that they are under my care, I can find out more about them. Their names. What they do for work. And why they are here on a Monday instead of a Friday. A good waitress can find out a lot about her customers without making it seem like she is prying or being too personal.

So that's all I have to do.

Be a good waitress. Smile. Serve.

And slip in a couple of questions, the answers to which are already causing me to salivate almost as much as the Murphys as they keep on reading those menus.

NADINE

It was my idea to go out for this meal on a Monday night. Part of the reason that I came to the decision was that it was my fault that we couldn't make it on Friday. But the other part is what is waiting for me in the morning. Tomorrow is when I will meet Kieran. And that is precisely why I needed something to take my mind off it tonight.

'Are you sure everything's okay?' Max asks me as I finish another glass of wine.

He's already asked me that question since we sat down at this table, and I know why he is so concerned. It's been impossible for him not to notice how fast and loose I am being with the wine in my glass.

How much have I had now? I'm not sure. All I know is that I'm not doing a very good job of sharing this bottle.

'How's your pizza?' I ask without answering his question.

'Er, yeah. It's okay.'

'Are you regretting not getting the meatballs?'

'No, this is good.'

'Okay then.'

I pick up my glass again, satisfied that I've just done my bit to fill the silence between us for a few seconds at least.

I feel bad for being a terrible conversationalist this evening, but it's impossible to be chatty with so much on my mind. All I can think about is Kieran. What I need to say to him. What he might say to me. And how things could be left between us when our meeting ends. The outcome will literally determine whether I have a family who loves me or a family who hates me, and I will have a better idea of which one it will be this time tomorrow.

I go back to stabbing at the pasta shells on my plate while Max tackles another slice of pizza, and it's almost too quiet again to be anything but awkward until somebody does speak at the table. It's Hannah, the waitress. She's back again to check on us, and like all the other times she has stopped by our table this evening, she is chatty and full of questions.

'Is everything okay with your meals?' she wants to know.

I nod my head and feel like that should be enough to send her on her way again, but Max decides to be just as chatty.

'It's great, thank you. I almost went with the meatballs, but I'm glad I chose the pizza.'

Why is he telling her that? Who cares? I'd say not Hannah, but I'm starting to think she actually does care. Is she really this nice all the time, or is she just desperate for a tip at the end?

I look up at the woman standing beside our table, and I can't help but feel like she is entirely unremarkable. The gold name badge pinned to her shirt is easily the most colourful thing about her. The rest of her is so plain and uninspiring.

The hair. The face. The posture beneath that uniform. All of it needs work. But then I notice one thing about her look that is definitely different to how she appeared when we first saw her this evening.

Her lips are red now, whereas before, they were pink and pale.

Has she applied lipstick since we got here? If so, why?

Perhaps her manager told her that she needed to make a bit more of an effort for the customers. Or maybe she decided herself that she needed to make the effort. But which customers spurred her into action? Max? Is she trying to impress him? All I know is that she is smiling at him now before she asks another question.

'You guys come here so much. I feel like it's bad if I just treat you like everybody else. What are your names?'

I'm just about to tell her that it is none of her business and send her on her way back to the bar for more wine, but once again, my husband speaks up and prolongs this whole thing.

'I'm Max, and this is Nadine,' he says, gesturing towards me. 'But don't worry about giving us any special treatment just because we come here a lot. We're no different to any of these other people.'

'Oh, don't put yourselves down. You're very valued customers, and it's nice to be able to put names to the faces now. As you can probably already see, my name is Hannah.'

'It's a pleasure to meet you properly, Hannah. And don't say this to Becki because I'd hate for her to be offended. But I have to say that the service this evening

83

has been much better than usual. Not that the other times were bad. But I hope you know what I mean.'

I'm looking at my husband like I have no idea what he means. Why is he still chattering away with this dowdy waitress when he could be talking to me? Sure, I've hardly been a font of conversation this evening, but still, I'm far more interesting than this woman could be.

Aren't I?

'That's okay, I won't tell Becki. But I understand what you mean. Perhaps the service is a little less personal on a Friday because it's so busy in here. Mondays are somewhat calmer, as you can tell.'

Hannah gestures around the half-empty room to make her point, but I keep my eyes on my smiling husband as he leans back in his seat.

'Well, maybe we'll have to start coming on Mondays instead then,' he suggests, and he then looks to me for my opinion on that. But I don't have one.

Bizarrely, Hannah doesn't leave the questions there, and by the time she has moved on from our table, she has managed to get Max to divulge what he does for a living and why we weren't here on Friday. He told her all about his business, information that she seemed to lap up, before he explained something had come up on Friday, and we were making up for it tonight. Neither my husband nor the waitress has any idea what actually 'came up' on Friday, which of course, I'm glad about, but what I'm not glad about is him chunnering away like he's talking to a long-lost friend. I make sure to tell him that once Hannah has finally gone.

'You shouldn't be so open with strangers.'

84

'What?'

'Telling her our names and what you do for work. It's none of her business.'

'She's just being nice.'

'Because she wants a tip.'

'So? It's her job. She's in hospitality.'

'It's not her job to pry.'

'I don't see what the problem is.'

'You never do.'

'What's that supposed to mean?'

'Nothing.'

I bite my tongue before saying any more. I'm in a foul mood because of all the stress of Kieran contacting Adam, and the looming meeting is weighing heavily on my mind. It was a bad idea to come here tonight and think I could distract myself from it. I just want to go home now, and I make that clear by telling Max that I'm far too full for dessert and that we should just get the bill.

He seems surprised, but I'm just grateful he doesn't want any dessert himself, and while it's tedious to have to listen to Hannah again as she brings us the bill and asks if we enjoyed our evening, it's a relief to be putting my coat on and heading for the door.

'I hope to see you two again soon,' Hannah says as we leave, and Max assures her that it won't be long until we are back. But I just keep my head down and say nothing, which is the same tactic I try and employ once we are in the car, driving home. The problem is, Max doesn't make it easy for me.

'Are you going to tell me what's going on, or am I going to have to prise it out of you like I had to do with the kids when they were younger?' Max asks as he navigates the dark roads.

'There's nothing wrong. I'm just tired.'

'You've barely said a word to me all night. You were rude to that waitress. And you still haven't told me what Friday night was all about.'

'I did tell you. Adam needed some food.'

'You seemed funny when you got back that night.'

'I was just tired from the drive.'

'Are you sure something didn't happen with Adam? Something more serious than him running out of food.'

'Of course, I'm sure.'

'You would tell me if there was something, wouldn't you? If he's struggling with his studies or whatever? Because he's my son too, you know.'

'I know he is!'

My voice went a little high then, but that's what happens when I'm forced into telling a lie during a heated discussion.

'So why were you grumpy tonight then?' Max goes on, thankfully dropping Adam and Friday night for now.

'I wasn't grumpy.'

'Yes, you were.'

I realise that I could carry on getting nowhere, or I could try and make this conversation a little more fun, if only to prevent us from having a fight and giving me one more problem to deal with. That's why I decide to start teasing my husband about the waitress.

'I might have been a little jealous at how friendly you were being with Hannah.'

'What?' Max says, clearly not expecting that.

'It felt like the two of you were flirting a little.'

I'm only being honest, and while I'm not that bothered if they were because I know Max would never be interested in another woman, especially one like her, I'm milking it to take the heat off what's really bugging me.

'We were not flirting!'

'Did you fancy her?'

'What? No way!'

'Are you sure about that? Perhaps you like the uniform? Or maybe it was her 'plain Jane' look. She's very different to me, but maybe that's what you want. Something different. A chance to slum it.'

'What are you talking about?'

'I'm only joking.'

Max's relief is palpable, and I decide to stop teasing him then now that the mood in the car is a little better than when the journey started. I also don't need him to try and convince me that I have nothing to worry about, but just before we get out of the car and go into our home, he does just that.

'You know I love you, right?' he says, and I nod my head because I do. 'And you know I feel bad about being away so much on business?'

I nod again.

'Well, I was thinking, there might be a way for me to be around a lot more.'

'Really?'

I would like that, although not tomorrow because I need Max out of the house, so he won't know I'm going out to meet the man who fathered one of our children.

'There have been a few offers from third parties interested in buying my company,' Max tells me. 'I've never considered them before because I was so focused on growing the business, but it's in a good place right now, and some of the offers are quite tempting.'

'What kind of offers?'

'Big ones.'

I'm surprised because I had never thought Max would sell the rights to the business that he had worked so hard to build. But those big offers must be big enough to make him contemplate it.

'I could retire. Be around more. We could travel. Go out for meals on any night of the week. Do whatever we want. Would you like that?'

'Of course I would. I'm just surprised.'

'We can think about it. We don't have to make any big decisions yet. I just thought I'd mention it. And I wanted to check that there wasn't anything wrong between us before I did.'

My heart aches at the thought of my hard-working, loyal and loving husband worrying that there was a rift developing between us. If there has been one, then it's all my fault, not his, and I feel so bad for potentially causing him to stress over it. I also feel bad if he feels like he has to give up his business to try and stop us from drifting further apart.

'I love you,' I tell him, taking his hand from where it was resting on the steering wheel and giving it a squeeze. 'And there's nothing wrong. I promise.'

I'm trying to be persuasive, and he sees that.

What he won't see is that tomorrow morning, I will be doing everything I can to persuade another man that everything is okay too.

Somehow, I think I will have a harder job on my hands the second time around.

HANNAH

This has been the best Monday in ages. That shift just seemed to fly by and my walk home did too. I didn't even contemplate calling in at the takeaway on the way back. Instead, it felt as though I skipped all the way to my house, and I did so with my mind filled with happy thoughts about the man at Table Six.

Max Murphy. I have his full name now. And I like it, just as I like him. He's friendly, chatty, confident. Polite, funny, composed. And he must like me too. Why else would he be so willing to talk to me and answer all my questions?

I was going to try and play it cool and not ask so much, but that didn't happen. Aware that it might have been my only time to serve the couple, I wanted to get as much information out of them as I could. Now I know that Max is the owner of a business. How cool. He must be loaded. He mentioned what exactly it was that he did. He invented some part for an air conditioning system that he now sells all around the country. But the details aren't the interesting bit. What's interesting is how open he was with me.

We chatted like we were two old friends, not just two people forced to interact in a constructed situation in society. I was his waitress, and he was my diner. We could easily have just kept to the basics.

'What do you want to order? Can I get you another drink? Here's the bill, thank you for your custom and have a lovely evening.'

But we didn't do that. I scratched beneath the surface, and we ended up going much deeper. Now I'm home in my boyfriend's house, yet all I can think about is Max and the answers he gave me.

And then there is his wife. The woman who sat opposite him and drank a lot of wine while saying very little. Nadine Murphy. I've admired her from afar for a long time. Her stylish clothes. Her lovely hair. The make-up that always seemed perfect. But now I have seen her up close, her personality has somewhat soured the pretty sight of her.

I don't know if she was mad at me, mad at Max or just mad at the world tonight. Whatever the reason for her foul mood, it was obvious she wasn't having as much fun as her husband was. Was that why he was so willing to talk to me? Because his wife wasn't talking to him. I'd like to think that he would have always been receptive to me, but it is possible he was just humouring himself with me while his wife stewed across the table for a reason that might not have been his fault.

The Murphys. They're not as much of a mystery after tonight, that's for sure. But they are still just as fascinating to me.

What isn't fascinating to me is this quiet, empty house. Being on my own here all the time is getting very old, very fast. I've just about had enough of being by myself. I think it's time for a change. I need a new man.

I need somebody like Max.

It's not hard for my mind to run away with itself as I entertain fantasies of sharing a home with him. Being the successful businessman he is, I bet we wouldn't want for anything. He'd want me to quit my job, of course, telling me that my days of slaving away for fussy diners were over and that it was time to put my feet up and let him do all the work. I'd protest for a short while just to be polite before excitedly handing in my notice at *San Bella* and hurrying back to Max to start planning all our adventures together.

He'd probably give me free reign on choosing the furniture and décor for our new place together. I'd leave him to all the serious jobs like managing the finances and the bills. But we would reconvene at the end of the day over a lovely dinner in our dining room. He'd tell me about his business deals that day. I would tell him what colour I have decided on in the second bathroom. And we would indulge in all the food and all the wine that Mrs Murphy doesn't seem to appreciate as much as I would.

What would become of her if she didn't have Max? If she was no longer Mrs Murphy? There's no real way of knowing for sure, but I'd have to assume she'd take losing her husband to another woman pretty badly, especially when that woman used to serve them dinner.

I bet Nadine has never seen me as a threat. But she has never seen me as a friend either, so I don't owe her anything. Who knows if I would be entertaining these thoughts of taking her man if she had been nicer to me? I'd like to think that I'd have been happy just being both of their friends, but if I'm honest, I know I would have always wanted more.

That's what I do. I keep pushing the boundaries until it's too much. And I would have done the same tonight if the Murphys had ordered dessert.

I would have asked more questions.

How long have they been married? Do they have kids? If so, what are their names?

I'd love to know more. I'd love to know everything.

And the more I get to know him, the more I start to love Max.

NADINE

I was wondering if I would recognise Kieran when I laid eyes on him. It has been a long time, after all. But there was no mistaking who he was when I saw him enter the pub and start walking towards me. Sure, he's aged, as have I, but he still carries himself with that same swagger that first attracted me to him. He was a cheeky chappy back then, and it'll be interesting to see if he has matured as he has grown into a man in middle age. But the most interesting thing that I can find out today is what it will take for him to leave Adam alone.

I set today's meeting place as The Rose and Crown, a watering hole in town that I haven't spent much time in, but that's exactly why I chose it. I wanted a place where nobody would know me. I just look like a woman meeting a man for a drink as lunchtime approaches on a boring, bland weekday.

No fuss. No attention. Nothing to see here.

I wish.

'You look well,' Kieran says to me when he reaches my table, and I'm not sure if he's expecting me to stand and offer him a hug for old time's sake. But I stay seated before telling him to put himself in the chair opposite me so that we can get down to business.

I had toyed with the idea of deploying a few tactics here today. Ask him how he's been. Show an interest. Convey some compassion. Perhaps that way, he would show me some compassion when I begged him to not ruin my life. But in the end, I have decided to just cut to the chase and get on with it.

'What can I offer you to leave Adam alone?' I say before Kieran has barely had time to get comfortable in his seat.

He seems surprised by my question, and it's probably for the best that the next question he hears is a much simpler one to answer.

'What can I get you?' the landlord of this pub asks after he has come out from behind the bar to check on the drinking needs of his two newest customers.

'A pint,' Kieran replies. 'Whatever you've got.'

'And for you, love?'

'Just a lemonade. Thank you.'

The barman goes to get our drinks as Kieran and I stare at each other and try to figure out what the other is thinking before we say it. We're like two chess players looking for an advantage, but it's still far too early in the game to get one. I have no idea what strategy my opponent wants to deploy yet.

'I've told you what I want,' Kieran says with a sigh. 'I want to meet my son. I want him to know the truth. Even if it doesn't go well for me, I just want him to know who I am.'

'What do you mean if it doesn't go well for you?' I say with a snarl. 'There's no ifs or buts about it. It will not go well. He will hate you. He will want to know why you didn't come forward sooner. And he will tell you to get lost.'

'You don't know that for sure.'

'Unlike you, I know my son.'

That was harsh, but it was also true. Kieran hasn't got a clue what Adam is like or how he might react to this news. I do because I've raised him. And now I have to shield my boy from danger again, just like when he was on the playground and a kid might have picked on him, or a big dog might have got too close and scared him.

'I've not come here to argue,' Kieran tries.

'And I've not come here to waste time. So, like I asked, what can I offer to make you leave Adam alone?'

'You think I want money?'

'I have no idea. But that is one option.'

'You've got to be joking. You think you can just pay me off to keep quiet as if there's any amount of money that would be worth more than my son.'

'Oh, quit trying to sound like the world's best dad and be honest. You ran away. You. Not Adam. He's always been here. But you haven't. So please stop pretending like you're some nobleman who is only interested in doing good deeds because we both know that's not true.'

We're interrupted then by the two drinks that are placed down on the table in between us, and there's a slightly awkward moment when the landlord asks for payment, and Kieran and I look at each other as if to say who is paying. I reach for my handbag to aid getting rid of the third party, but Kieran gets his wallet out quicker and taps his card on the machine to cover our debt to this publican. Then we are alone again, and I take the chance to keep the theme of money running while it's fresh in both our minds.

'I'm not sure if you are aware, but my husband is doing very well for himself these days. So if it is money you want, I can get you plenty of it. It might take me a little time, but it's there.'

'I just told you that I'm not interested in money.'

'And why is that? What exactly is that you do for work these days?'

'That's not got anything to do with it.'

'Whatever it is, I doubt it's as highly paid as Max is. So come on, stop messing around and name your price. All cowards have one. So let's hear yours.'

'I knew this was going to be a waste of time.'

Kieran goes to get up then, and I fear I've played this all wrong. To show my remorse, I reach out and grab his arm, a strong sign that he holds all the power here and not me, despite how I've been trying to make things look since he got here.

'Please. Don't go. I really want us to sort this out.'

Kieran looks at my hand, gripping his arm for a moment before giving in and easing back into his seat before he takes a long sip of his frothy ale and licks his lips. Annoyingly, he seems to be growing more confident while I feel like I'm already floundering. And to prove it, I wait for him to speak next.

'What if the thing I want is something else? Not money. Something more personal.'

'Like what?'

'You.'

'What?'

I hadn't been sure if the offer of cold, hard cash was going to work, but one thing I had not been counting on was for Kieran to counter with an indecent proposal like he has.

'One night with you. For old time's sake. Then I'll go away. How about it?'

I feel sick, but even so, part of me is feeling hopeful that there is a way out of this mess without my son screaming at me and Max throwing me out of our house.

'Erm, okay. If that's what you want,' I say, my mind scanning through all the options of how we could make it work and keep it a secret. But before I've finished doing the sums, Kieran breaks out into a loud laugh, and that's when I realise that he was joking.

'You bastard,' I say as my stomach churns. That initial wave of relief that I won't have to sleep with him again has quickly been replaced by the realisation that I'm still very much screwed now, regardless.

'I'm sorry,' Kieran says. 'But you weren't taking this seriously, so why should I?'

'I am taking this very seriously,' I say, raising my voice and leaning across the table to further emphasise my point. 'I will do anything to get you to disappear again. I just want to know what you want, and don't say Adam because you've never wanted him.'

'We're wasting our time here,' Kieran says as he drains more of his pint and looks like he might be ready to try and leave again.

'Please. I urge you to reconsider. Like I said, I have money.'

'No, you have your husband's money, which I imagine won't be the case for very long once he finds out that his son is not really his.'

'You can't do this to my husband. It will kill him.'

'You're the one who did it.'

'Please, Kieran. Please!'

I can't control the tears that have filled up my eyes, and even though I wipe them away, it's too late for Kieran not to see them. Getting upset seems like a huge display of weakness, but then I wonder if my vulnerability could work in my favour. I'll cry rivers if it gets this man to see things from my point of view and back down.

Amazingly, it seems to work because the man opposite me softens, and he stares into his pint glass before speaking again.

'How much money would we be talking about here?' he asks me as I dab at my eyes with a tissue from my handbag. 'Just out of interest.'

'I will pay anything to keep my family together.'

'A million?'

The tears dry pretty quickly in the face of such a figure, although my bank manager might well be crying if I ask him for such a deposit.

'Wow, that much?' I ask, hoping he might be joking with me again. But this time, he is deadly serious.

'If you're asking if there is any amount of money that could make me walk away from Adam, then that is the figure.'

I swallow hard and try not to look too shocked, but I'm sure all the colour must have drained from my face. Do we have a million pounds to hand? Possibly. We'll definitely have it if Max sells his business like he suggested last night. But the money isn't the real problem. The real problem is withdrawing it and giving it to Kieran without Max finding out.

'I'm going to need some time,' I say after taking several seconds just to figure that out.

'How much time?'

'I don't know, but you've just asked me for a lot of money, so give me a chance.'

'Fair enough. But don't take too long. I might change my mind. I know it might seem like I'm choosing money over my boy, but I do love him, and I do regret what I did. So, the longer you keep me waiting, the more chance there is that I don't want the money anymore.'

Kieran finishes his pint then and stands up to leave, but I make sure to establish a few ground rules before he does.

'If I do this, I want a guarantee that you won't ever come back again.'

'What do you mean?'

'I'll have a lawyer draw up a contract. A restraining order. Whatever it takes. Something to make it illegal for you to ever bother me or my son again.'

Kieran thinks about it for a moment before nodding his head.

'That sounds fair enough. But don't get too distracted. You've got a lot of money to get hold of, and you haven't got all the time in the world. So, one job at a time, hey?'

With that, Kieran walks away, and I'm left sitting in the corner of this pokey pub, nursing a full glass of lemonade and wondering how the mistakes I made in my life have led me to this very moment right here.

Kieran is right. One job at a time. I've kept the wolf from the door for now.

The next thing on the To-Do list is to try and slip seven figures past my husband without him noticing.

HANNAH

I got engaged when I was twenty-seven. His name was Zach, and I met him in the pub that I was working in as a barmaid at the time. I was used to spending most of my day serving old men with flat caps on their heads and newspapers under their arms, or football fans who would break into various chants after a couple of drinks and needed me to remind them to keep the noise down. Therefore, it was quite a nice change to one day be tasked with serving the quiet, handsome, debonair man who came in by himself and ordered a vodka and coke.

While Zach was easy on the eye, the thing that drew me to him the most was how nervous he seemed. I was curious, so I asked him if everything was okay once I had furnished him with his beverage, and that had been when he had told me that he was getting ready for a first date in a pub up the street. It turned out that he had come into my workplace to try and calm some of those nerves with a little help from Mr Grey Goose.

I thought it was sweet that he was anxious about his date, but I was also a little envious that this man would be getting to sit down and talk with someone else tonight who wasn't me. But that was when I realised that I was at a distinct advantage to my 'love rival', who hadn't had the chance to have her date with Zach yet. The advantage was that he was with me, not her, and as long as I kept him in my pub, he couldn't go and meet her in that other one.

Bear in mind this was over ten years ago, so I was a lot better looking then than I am now. I was slimmer, sassier and dare I say it, sexier. All I had to do was make sure that Zach saw that too.

Laying on the charm, along with a little help from the extra button on my blouse that I had undone, I made sure Zach was kept busy chatting to me for so long that his date started to pale into insignificance. I flirted, I found everything he said ten times funnier than it was, and I managed to sneak him a couple of free drinks to the point where his nerves melted away, and he was very receptive to my charms. In the end, it was a forgone conclusion that he was going to cancel his date at the last minute and spend the rest of the night with me.

From those humble beginnings, ours was a love that blossomed into something very serious. We met each other's friends. We moved in together. And then we began to plan for marriage when he popped the question during a weekend getaway in Devon.

I loved being a fiancée. It was basically several months of getting to get together with my girlfriends and talk them through all of my plans. The venues I was looking at. The dresses I had my eye on. And the ideas for our honeymoon, all of which were very exotic. I also liked it because it was around that time that my friends were either married or getting engaged, so it was a lot easier to fit in with them when I was no longer the only singleton in the group.

So what happened? Where was my happy ending? Why, a decade on, have I ended up as a waitress lusting over a married man who comes in every Friday instead of being settled with a ring on my finger and a couple of kids to bring up?

Simple. Zach cheated on me. But he didn't just do it with anybody.

He did so with one of my best friends.

That group of girlfriends I had? They weren't so great when one of them stabs you in the back, and the others are so mortified that they can never be themselves around you again.

I called off the wedding and got rid of Zach immediately, and surprisingly, that was the easy part. The hard part was realising that I was too embarrassed to be around my friends after that. They were all settling down and starting families with loyal men by their side, while it felt like I was cast aside onto the scrap heap of life. I was still young, but that didn't matter because I didn't want to start again. I thought I'd found my future, and I was set for life. But I was wrong.

So very, very wrong.

Being single sucked. Being broke was just as bad, but that's what happened when I stopped turning up for my shifts in the pub. I couldn't face anybody. I felt like everyone was laughing at me, even complete strangers who had no idea what I had been through. In the end, I did the only thing I could.

I left my hometown, and I didn't look back.

I thought time would heal the wounds. I thought I'd fall in love again and not be paranoid about getting hurt a second time. And I thought I'd make new friends in a new place once I was comfortable opening myself up to a different group of women. But instead, I felt myself becoming angrier, more bitter and more twisted. The years ticked by, and things weren't getting any better. Just a series of dead-end jobs interspersed with me getting my hopes up about a guy, only to find out he wasn't interested in me. That was why I stopped making an effort with my appearance. I put on a bit of weight and went half the week without make-up. Nobody cared. Nobody told me to sort myself out. I just faded into the background while everyone else got to experience all the things I had missed out on.

One day, three years ago now, I decided to look up Zach and see what he was doing. The internet makes it easy to find out about other people from a safe distance, and that's what I did with the man who had betrayed me. I discovered he was married, had three kids (three!), and he even had a dog that made me feel sick because he was the cutest little thing I'd ever seen, and I hated him for that. It seemed that despite what he had done, life had worked out pretty well for Zach.

I wish I could say that I left it there. I wish I could say that I put my phone away and got on with my life without giving him a second thought. But I didn't. I ended up becoming obsessed with that perfect family of his, and that was what led me back to my hometown. His LinkedIn page told me where he worked, and after waiting outside his office to see him leave, I followed him home.

And what a home it was.

Detached. Must have had at least four bedrooms. And in an area where crime was just some strange word the residents occasionally overheard on the news while they left their doors unlocked and their house alarms deactivated.

It was the perfect place for the imperfect man.

So that was why I knocked on the door.

I wanted to give Zach's new partner a tip-off about the man she had a family with. The man she trusted. The man she surely had no idea was capable of ripping out someone's heart only weeks out from their wedding day.

It was Zach who answered. It actually took him a moment to recognise me. When he did, he didn't look shocked. He looked sad, and that was almost worse. The pity seemed to be emanating off him in waves.

But that soon stopped when his wife appeared in the doorway behind him.

I just blurted it out. Said I was Zach's ex-fiancée, and he had broken my heart after sleeping with one of my most trusted friends. I told them that my life was a mess, and it was all his fault. And then I waited to see what either of them had to say about that.

It turned out that it was not a lot.

I wish they had got angry, upset, or just done something that might have made them feel as bad as I was feeling. But that's not what happened. Why? Because it turned out that Zach had already told his new partner what he had done in his past. Therefore, what I had said had not come as a shock. That's why I didn't get the response I was looking for. Instead, I just got that awful thing again.

Pity.

And lots of it.

I ran away from that house after realising that it had been a mistake to go there, and I've never been back to my hometown since. Going back there was a mistake because it taught me many things, not least of which was that life is not so much about heroes and villains, but more about a series of highs and lows that ultimately end up making no difference in the grand scheme of things.

Zach wasn't the bad guy. He just made a mistake. And I wasn't innocent, as I would later go on to prove with what came next in my life.

I wish I hadn't had to learn those things, but I did, and I learned them the hard way.

That's why love is a very dangerous thing for me to indulge in.

It's now why Nadine needs to keep a very serious eye on her husband.

NADINE

I'm in a fortunate position where a million pounds is not completely out of reach for me. But I'm in the unfortunate position of having to access it without anybody else knowing.

I wish I could just withdraw the cash, throw it into a bag, hand it to Kieran and say good riddance. Sure, losing such a sum would sting, but if that's the price to keep my family together, then so be it. But it's not as simple as that. I might be one of my bank's favourite customers due to the numbers in my account and the mortgage my husband applied for, but there are still systems in place. All sorts of checks and balances. This isn't the Wild West. Withdrawing seven figures in one fell swoop these days would be almost akin to holding up a bank with a gun and demanding the clerk stay calm, so nobody gets hurt.

They'd want to know why I needed the money. What I planned on spending it on. And they might even want to consult my husband, who happens to also be named on all my accounts because we've done everything together ever since we married.

But there is another way.

Max is planning on selling the business. With the funds that will raise, it would make it a little easier for such a large sum of money to 'go missing.' The bank manager, and my husband, might not be so intrigued to know where a million was going if there were several millions still sitting in the bank. I could set up a new account. Move the money. Tell Max I had found some super high savings account to store it in. And maybe one day, in time, he'd forget I ever took it as he focused on spending all the other money he had earned through the sale of his brilliant business.

One thing is for sure, without the sale of his company, I won't be able to get that money.

I only hope Kieran can be patient until that happens.

I've drifted between incredibly positive highs, in which I think everything will be okay, and soul-crushing lows, when I suddenly fear that it won't be. That's just today, and it's not even dinner time yet. But in general, I'm feeling more on the optimistic side, and that's because I've managed to keep a secret from Max for so long. Therefore, I feel like I can do it again, and this time, it will be the last one.

But then Max came home after another busy day and said something I did not want to hear.

'I've been thinking,' he began, a sentence which never seems to end well for the person on the receiving end of it. 'I'm not sure I'm going to sell the business.'

I actually stopped breathing when he said it.

'What?' was all I could choke out after several seconds.

'I mean, sure, the money would be great. But what would I do all day once the novelty of it all had worn off? I'd get bored without a purpose.'

'But you were adamant that you wanted to retire the other day!'

'I know, but I've given it more thought, and I'm not sure it's for the best. I mean, I'm in my early forties. How many people retire that young?'

'But not many people have created a business worth millions!'

It must sound like I am bigging up my resourceful partner, but I'm really just trying to say anything to get him to stick to the original plan.

Retire. Sell for millions. *And allow me to skim a million off the top to pay Kieran.*

'You hear all those stories of people who retired and suddenly found themselves with nothing to do. They were dead within six months. As if their bodies just gave up because there was nothing to get them out of bed in the mornings. What if it's not healthy to just suddenly stop?'

'This is different.'

'Is it?'

'Yes. You're not like everyone else.'

'I always thought that too. But now I'm not so sure. If I do this, I'll just be another person who used to work hard but now just plays golf all day and falls asleep in front of daytime TV.'

'You hate golf. And TV. You'll find something else to do. And like you said, we can spend more time together. I'll keep you busy, don't worry about that.'

I smile to try and snap Max out of his concerning train of thought, and thankfully, it seems to do the trick.

'Maybe you're right. I guess it's just the fear of the unknown.'

'Don't worry about that. It's the fear of giving me a hand with some of the housework that should really bother you.'

Max laughs as I give him a hug, and it feels good to feel him squeezing me as we embrace. I need every ounce of strength I can get to make it through this troubling time, and I don't have enough of it on my own. I could use some of my partners, too.

The next hour passes a lot more easily, and Max doesn't mention pulling out of the sale again, leaving me to think that I might still have a way out of my mess after all. Then it's time to sit down because we have a couple of important video calls planned this evening. Firstly, we are checking in with Sophie out in Asia, and then it will be time for a quick chat with Adam at university.

I insisted on both of them making the time to connect with home this evening because I knew Max was going to be home a little earlier, and it's already been a while since he got to hear from them both. It's important the family stays connected now we're all spread around, but there's another reason why I scheduled these calls tonight. I know that Max will mention his news about the possible sale to gauge his children's reaction, and when he does, I know what they will say.

Do it, Dad. Life's too short.

Sell. Travel.

And don't forget to give me some of the money.

Their reaction will stiffen his resolve, and soon, those millions will be flowing to us, giving me the opportunity to divert some of it towards the man I need gone.

The first call with Sophie goes as expected. She's in an internet café in Phuket, and while the connection isn't great, her reaction to her father's news is. As I'd hoped, she urges Max to sell, telling him she is so proud of how hard he has worked, before adding that if possible, she could do with a little more money being sent over because she quite fancies the idea of going to Sri Lanka soon.

After an enjoyable half an hour with our daughter, it's time for Adam's face to appear on our laptop screen, and when he does, I instantly feel a pang of guilt. That's because of how Max reacts to seeing 'his' boy for the first time in a while.

He's beaming. He's excited. And he's almost living vicariously through him as he laps up all the tales of Adam's nights out, his new friends and that mystery girl we have seen him tagged in photos with recently. The subject of actual coursework is conspicuous by its absence, but we both let that slide as we watch and listen to our excited boy assure us that he is having fun but will definitely be back for the Christmas holidays as planned.

When the calls are finished and the sound of youthful chatter has left our home once more, it's back to just Max and me, the couple who raised those two adventurous young adults who are now out there making their mark in the world. That must be why Max is smiling at me as he shakes his head and says he can't believe how grown up our kids are now. I can't believe it either, but it's not just a throwaway remark on my husband's behalf. I see that he actually has tears in his eyes. But he's not upset. He's proud.

He loves his kids so much.

And that is why I have to do anything to keep him thinking that they are *both* his kids.

Whatever it takes to not break his heart.

'You're definitely going to sell?' I ask one more time as we get into bed an hour later.

'Yeah, definitely,' Max replies as he settles onto his pillow.

That's it decided then.

He's getting a big payout.

And so is Kieran.

HANNAH

Before the Murphys came The Spinners. They didn't stick to a weekly routine like Max and Nadine, but they did visit *San Bella* regularly. At least once a month, sometimes twice. But they didn't care which table they sat at. It could be Table Six by the window or Table Two by the door, or maybe even Table Fourteen near the kitchen. It didn't matter. They were happy to sit anywhere and, in the case of Mr Spinner, happy to chat with the staff when they were here.

I was first attracted to Michael when I saw him walk in. Tall, handsome, well dressed. He wasn't hard to fancy. But what really made me like him was how outgoing he was. He asked me how my night was going when I served them, instead of just leaving it to the waitress to do all the work. He asked for my opinion on certain dishes and even complimented me on my skills when carrying several plates away from his table.

He was friendly, flirty and fun, and he had me under his spell.

But then I realised that he was just like that with everybody. It didn't matter which waitress he had, he treated them all the same. That's when I realised that I wasn't special. He was clearly just a guy who was comfortable in the presence of the opposite sex and was so confident that he didn't even seem to tone his flirting down despite his wife sitting opposite him. But she didn't mind. If anything, she almost seemed to enjoy it, and at the time, I suspected that was because despite all

114

his flirting, she knew she was the one who the handsome man was going home with.

But after learning that I was not unique, I started to resent the fact that I would never have him. It used to bother me that he could be like he was with any woman, not just me. But then I learnt that he wasn't just the flirty type. He actually took more action than that, and I discovered that fact one evening after he had come to the restaurant alone. I saw one of the waitresses getting into his car at the end of our shift, and while everybody else either ignored it or found it funny, I was mortified.

How could he do that? How could he cheat on his wife?

But more importantly, if he was going to cheat, why wasn't he cheating with me?

I waited until he was in the restaurant again before I made my move. After 'accidentally' knocking his suit jacket off the back of his chair, I was able to remove his wallet discreetly and take out his driving licence once in the safety of the staff toilets. I was able to casually drop the wallet behind his chair when I passed through the restaurant again, leaving him to assume it just fell out of his jacket when he discovered it on the floor. But I still had his I.D. with his address on it in my possession. Then all I had to do was visit his home when I was off-duty and wait for him to be by himself.

Having watched his wife leave in her brilliant blue sports car, I had knocked on the door of the impressive home and waited for the man of the house to answer. When he had, Michael had been wearing a gym vest and a pair of shorts and looked like he was

115

sweating. I would later find out that he had just completed a workout in his expansive home gym.

Michael was loaded. But that wasn't why I was there.

I didn't care about his money.

I just wanted him to want me.

After producing his driving licence and telling him it must have fallen out of his wallet at the restaurant, he seemed happier to see me, and he only warmed to my presence even more when I complimented him on his physique. I made it obvious that I was attracted to him and that, coupled with the fact his wife was out of the house, made it easier for me to persuade him that I could come inside.

We slept together. It was hurried and urgent and not quite how I had imagined it going, but it happened all the same. I had gotten what I wanted.

Almost.

Having been intimate with Michael, it only made me want to be around him more, and after what we had done together, I had hoped he might be feeling the same way. Could we somehow make it work? Would he leave his wife for me? Was this the happy future to make up for my unhappy past?

In a word, no.

Michael didn't leave his wife for me. He had no intention of doing such a thing. It was obvious that I was just another one of his flings. Nothing more, nothing less. To make it even worse, he barely acknowledged me the next time he came into the restaurant. He acted as if I wasn't the woman who had been in his bed the week before. He deserved an Oscar for the way he so casually ordered his dessert with me while his wife sat opposite him being none the wiser as to who I really was and what I had done with her man.

I blame what happened next on Michael's nonchalance. If only he had been more respectful to me, then I like to think that I wouldn't have gone back to his house. But I did go back. Only that time, I went back when he was out, and his wife was home alone.

Victoria Spinner was not shocked when I told her she was married to a cheat. In fact, it was quite the opposite. She rolled her eyes and shrugged her shoulders as if I had just told her that it might rain tomorrow, not that the man who had put a ring on her finger had slept with me in their marital bed. It turned out that she knew all about her partner's penchant for other women and was not at all fussed by it. She called me another one of his "floozys" and said she was with him for the money and not his ability to keep it in his trousers. I even got the impression she engaged in a little extra-marital activity herself.

But that was not what I had wanted to hear. I wanted Victoria to be mad. To hate her husband. And to be on my side. For her to agree with me that all men are rotten and that they don't deserve people like us. Most of all, I wanted to feel as though Victoria knew how I felt all those years ago when my fiancé had cheated on me.

It didn't go that way, however. Victoria just laughed at me and asked me to leave. So I got angry and picked up the nearest thing to hand, which happened to be a vase full of flowers that was sitting on the hallway table. The flowers weren't much use but their receptacle was, and as the vase crashed down over Victoria's head, she finally stopped laughing at me.

She also stopped moving.

I'd killed her. In her own home. All because I got involved with her husband.

Michael.

I knew he would come home and discover his partner lying on the hallway floor and when he did, he would surely call the police. Would I get caught for this? I didn't know. All I knew was that I wanted to prevent that 999 call for as long as possible.

That was why I waited for Michael to come home, hiding in the hallway so I would be behind the front door when it opened. It took a while, but the man of the house eventually came back.

He saw his wife lying on the floor where I had left it.

But that was the last thing he saw before I killed him too.

Unable to use the vase that was now in several pieces around the body of Victoria, I had opted to take a knife from the kitchen. It was a very harsh and brutal way for Michael to go, but I had to do whatever it took to prevent him from calling the police.

I left after that. Went home and tried to act like I hadn't just killed two people. It wasn't easy. That next shift at *San Bella* was the hardest one I've ever been through. But I managed it, and by the time the news began to filter through that two people had been found bludgeoned to death in their home, I was feeling confident that I could get away with it as long as I stayed calm.

So that's what I did.

I have stayed calm for these last two years.

Until now.

I have another man in my sights again.

And just like Michael, he is married too.

Does that mean I want the same outcome for the Murphys as the Spinners? No, of course not. I feel terrible for putting two people in an early grave, and I would hate for it to happen again.

This time has to be different.

This time, there can be no mistakes.

This time, I have to get my man.

NADINE

The sale of Max's business is going through but not quickly enough for the funds to hit our account. That's why I've had to take a risk. I'm calling Kieran now to tell him that I can get him a portion of his money, but he will have to wait a little while for the rest of it.

I hope he will agree to it. I'm hardly giving him an insignificant sum. But it's not the full figure we agreed on, and I am aware he might be upset by that.

My nerves are jangling as I wait for Kieran to pick up the phone so I can give him the news. When he answers, he sounds strangely calm, as if he is not a man who is desperately waiting to be furnished with a life-changing amount of money.

'Kieran. Hi. Thanks for picking up.'

I've decided to be as nice as I can to him in the hope that it will soften the blow of only having some of his cash to hand at present.

'Do you have it?' he asks me, cutting straight to the chase.

'That's what I'm calling you about. You know I told you Max was selling his company. Well, it's going to take some time, so I can't get you all of the money yet. But I have some of it.'

'How much?'

'Seventy-two thousand.'

I was hoping for some sympathy or acknowledgement of the reasonably sized sum, but I don't get it. I don't even get silence. Instead, I just hear laughter.

'I should have known you weren't taking me seriously,' Kieran says after he has composed himself. 'I knew this was a waste of time.'

'No, I am taking this seriously! I am! I will get you your money. All of it! I just need more time.'

'You're deliberately stalling, hoping I'll just go away.'

'No, I'm not! I swear!'

This isn't going as well as I had hoped it might, and I feel like I'm losing the man at the other end of the line.

'Please, just give me more time.'

'Guess where I am.'

The strange teaser from Kieran comes out of the blue and only causes my anxiety to rachet up.

'Where?'

'I'm walking around a university campus. Would you care to guess which one?'

He's at Adam's uni? Oh my God, no.

'What are you doing? This isn't what we agreed?'

'I'm not the only one who isn't sticking to the plan, am I?'

'Kieran, please! Don't go to see Adam!'

'There are so many people around. Students. Lecturers. A few parents. Finding Adam would almost be like looking for a needle in a haystack. If only I knew exactly where to look.'

'Kieran, please!'

'I'm looking at him right now, you know?' Kieran tells me, and a freezing cold bolt of energy surges through me, making me wish I could travel down this phone line and be on that campus now to drag Kieran away before he can get to my boy.

'You promised me you wouldn't do this! We had a deal!'

'You don't have my money, so the deal is off.'

'I will get it. Just give me more time!'

'Time's up.'

'No!'

I'm aware then that Kieran could just end the call, and there would be no way for me to stop him walking up to Adam and telling him the truth before I have a chance to make contact with my son. That thought is easily the scariest thing I've ever had to contemplate, and that's why I have to do anything I can to keep Kieran on the phone.

'More money! I'll give you more money! Just don't do this! Please.'

Kieran is quiet, but I can still hear background noise at his end, so he hasn't hung up yet. I've bought myself a little more time, even if it could prove to be very costly.

'Wow, you really will do anything to keep your secret, won't you?'

'Yes, anything!'

'Anything but do the right thing and tell the truth.'

'What?'

The sudden change in tone in Kieran's voice only makes that anxious ball of despair in my stomach grow larger.

122

'I've changed my mind about the money. I don't want it. I want a relationship with my son. That's more important to me at this stage of my life.'

'But you agreed! We had a deal!'

'The deal's off. I'm sorry, but I can't do it. I can't walk away knowing I didn't even try.'

'Kieran, no! Don't do this!'

'Adam is with some friends. I can see them all through this window. He hasn't seen me out here yet, but I could just go inside and talk to him.'

'Don't! You'll ruin his life!'

'His or yours?'

'Both!'

I'm almost regretting not getting into my car as soon as this conversation started going south because at least I could have been a couple of minutes closer to the university by now. Not that it would have made much of a difference if Kieran is hellbent on talking to Adam today.

But then he throws me a lifeline.

'This isn't fair. You're right. I changed the plan. That's why I'm going to give you one last chance. You have twenty-four hours to tell your son the truth. Or I will do it, and this will be over.'

Kieran hangs up then, and I scream at my phone before trying to call him back. But he doesn't answer again, and my imagination can only run wild as I picture him so close to my son on campus. This is it. It's really happening. My worst nightmare is coming true.

And there's nothing I can do to stop it.

HANNAH

Another long, dreary shift, this one only brightened briefly by the slice of pizza I had on my break. It was leftovers from the extra food the chefs make for the staff to enjoy, and while I don't usually indulge, I did today. I needed the carbs, and I needed the few seconds of pleasure it gave me.

Lord knows it's been a long time since I had much of that.

Now I'm back on the restaurant floor and forced into serving the solitary man at the table in the middle of the room. I've seen him here before. He always comes alone, and he always chats to me when he's here. It's been a while, but he's back, and that means I have to put up with him again. But that's a bit of a chore because he's not half as handsome as Max Murphy, nor is he in any way as charming. But he is a customer, and I'm always under the watchful eye of the management team here, so I smile and serve him just as well as if he was the man I am lusting after now.

'What's the matter, dear?' the lone diner asks me rather unexpectedly as I'm removing his empty plate after his main course is over.

'I'm sorry?'

'I've just noticed you're looking a little glum this evening. Is everything alright?'

'I'm fine.'

'I hope they're not working you too hard here.'

'They're not.'

'It's just that I've been coming here a while, and I've noticed you definitely do a lot more than the other waitresses. I admire your work ethic, and I only hope your boss does too.'

'Erm, I'm not sure he does. But thank you.'

I'm ready to leave then, but before I go, the man says my name.

'Hannah. Very pretty name. Would you like to know mine?'

Once again, the presence of a name badge on my uniform seems to have caused another diner to feel as they know me better than they do. Instead of just being some waitress who operates in the background, the displaying of my name seems to make some folk think that I'm their friend.

I like Max knowing my name. But I don't really want anyone else to know it. Not with what I've done in the past. The fewer people who know about me, the better.

'My name is Tom,' the man says after I have failed to answer his question.

'Oh, okay.'

'I felt bad having you serve me so often and not knowing who I was while I knew who you were.'

I feel like telling Tom that he has absolutely no idea who I am, not really, but I don't because that wouldn't be wise. I just smile and plan on walking away again. But then Tom really surprises me.

'I was wondering if you would like to go for a drink with me,' he says with hope in his eyes and a slightly awkward smile. 'Or dinner, perhaps. Although I appreciate spending your free time in a restaurant might not feel like much of a break for you.'

I'm stunned. Have I just been asked out on a date? It seems that way. I'm so out of practise that I almost don't know what to do. *Almost.* But I do know. I have to say no. Turn Tom down. I have to do that because Max is the man for me, and it wouldn't be right for me to be seeing anybody else. I've already got rid of my last boyfriend so that I'm single and ready for him. Tom will only get in the way of things.

'I'm sorry. I'm very flattered, but I'm seeing somebody,' I say, hoping he buys my lie and leaves it at that.

'Oh, I see. That's a pity.'

Tom looks disappointed, and I feel bad for him for a moment, but this is just how affairs of the heart are. They're never simple, and they don't always go to plan. But I'm sure Tom will survive. He probably only asked me because he's lonely.

'I'll be right back with the dessert menu,' I tell him before I finally get away from his table and make it back into the kitchen, my head spinning a little at the surprise invitation. I wonder if that was what has kept him coming back here. Is it because of me? Will he stop coming now I've turned him down? Or will he just have a go with one of the other waitresses? I already know that I'm nothing special, so I fully expect to see Tom already chatting up one of the other employees when I leave the kitchen and return to the restaurant floor.

But I don't see that. I just see Tom sitting alone and staring mournfully out of the window at the dark sky outside.

The rest of my shift passes without incident, and I make sure to wish Tom a good night as he departs the restaurant. I hurry home myself when it's time to leave, but just as I reach the house, I see something that causes me to pause.

There's a light on inside.

Someone's here.

So I can't go in.

Loitering outside in the bushes at the back of the house, I keep watch as I see a figure move past one of the windows upstairs. I see several more lights going on and off before the figure is downstairs, standing in front of the kitchen window and looking out. But I know they can't see me. I'm well-hidden here. But I am cold, and I don't want to be standing out here all night, so I really wish they would leave so I can go in.

It takes another ten minutes but eventually, I see the last light go off in the house before the sound of a car engine on the driveway lets me know the visitor is definitely departing. But I stay hidden for ten more minutes just to make sure they are really gone before I go in and can finally relax after my shift.

I get inside the house as I always do, using the key from under the plant pot. I don't have to worry about the alarm because I learnt the code to that a long time ago. And it doesn't take me long to take out the pillow and the duvet from the back of the airing cupboard, the one that still contains towels and bed linen owned by the previous owners.

The person who was just inside this house will have had no idea I have been living here, as always. If they did, they would be furious. They would call the police. And then they might have half a chance at discovering that I am the person who killed the previous occupants.

This is Michael and Victoria's house. I've been living here secretly since I noticed the property was sitting empty after their deaths, and Michael's parents were in no rush to sell it. Their understandable lack of desire to cash in on their deceased son's bricks and mortar was my opportunity to live somewhere far above my means. A big house devoid of furniture is still better than a small flat filled with crummy things.

If it seems crazy to return to the scene of the crime, then understand that I couldn't just forget about Michael, even when he was dead, and I was standing with his blood pooling at my feet. In my head, he has been my boyfriend for the last two years. I just told myself he was working away a lot. I know it's sad, but it was the only way I could keep going through all those long, miserable shifts at the restaurant. I've learnt that life is better when I'm in love with someone, even if that someone is no longer alive.

But now I have Max. I can move on from Michael. I'm hoping I will be living with him very soon, and then I can leave this house of horrors behind. I'm starting to get sick of having to creep around and keep the lights off, as well as sleeping on the carpet and sneaking around in the bushes if Michael's parents are here. They don't come very often, but I still have to be on my guard, making sure to remove all evidence of my stay before I leave every day.

I got in the front door by watching Michael's parents put a key under the plant pot in the days after their son's death. I learnt the access code after finding a four-digit sequence scribbled on a piece of paper in a drawer in the kitchen when I was looking for the knife that I stabbed Michael with. And I've managed to live here undetected through a combination of luck and skill ever since.

But now it's time to flourish again, instead of being a wallflower.

Max can help me forget the pain of my past.

And guess what tomorrow is?

Friday.

HANNAH

It's 19:30. And there's no sign of the Murphys at *San Bella*.

Come on, where are you? Don't do this to me. I need to see you this week, Max.

'What are you doing?'

I look up from the reservation book to see my manager glaring at me.

'Sorry. I was just checking if Table Six are still booked in.'

'Yes, they are. Now get back to work.'

I rush back onto the restaurant floor, returning to doing what I'm paid to do here instead of dithering by the door and hoping to see Max.

If the Murphys are coming, then they're late. If they're not coming, then this is going to be a very bad night, not least because Tom is in again, and he's always got his eyes on me whenever I move across the room.

But then I see the man I'm looking for.

Max.

He is here.

But he's alone.

I can see Becki has already been summoned to seat him, and I watch as she leads him to the familiar table by the window. But despite not being his official waitress this evening, there is no way I'm not going to talk to Max at some point tonight.

My shift continues as normal, and I watch as Max orders his drinks and his starter, but it's around the midway point of his meal when I see an opportunity to

130

get closer to him. Max's main course is sitting on the pass, that area of the kitchen where the plates that are ready to be served sit under the hot lights for the waitresses to take. Becki should be springing into action now to prevent the perfectly cooked meal getting cold, but she isn't. She's too busy looking at her phone, which she shouldn't have on her during her shift, but she's never been one to worry about the rules. It would usually bother me but not tonight. Not when I can take Max's meal instead of her.

'I've got it,' I say as I pick up Max's plate and head for the door, and Becki barely looks up from her device as I pass her, not even thanking me for doing the thing she should be doing.

Reaching Max's table, I notice that he is looking a little forlorn, and I want to get to the bottom of that right away.

'Hi,' I say, making sure to put on my biggest and best smile as he sees me. 'Here's your main course.'

I drop the plate down on the table in front of him, and he thanks me. But I'm not done yet.

'Is everything okay? I notice you're not here with your wife.'

'Oh, erm. Yeah. She's fine. She's just feeling a little under the weather this evening.'

'Oh, that's a shame. I hope she's better soon.'

'Thank you.'

'Yeah, it's never as much fun eating alone, is it?'

'No, not quite.'

131

'Well, don't worry. I'm always happy to chat if you need some company. When I'm not serving these other tables, of course.'

Max smiles, and I'm doing a good job of getting him to like me even more.

'Didn't you think about cancelling?' I ask, curious as to why Max decided to come here alone. Was it to see me? That might be wishful thinking, but it won't hurt to ask.

'I was going to, but my wife insisted that I come. She told me I'd been working so hard recently that I deserved it. And she also told me she wasn't well enough to cook, so it was either this or a dodgy takeaway.'

I laugh before focusing on the nugget of information he gave me about his work.

'Is everything going well with your business?' I ask, demonstrating to him that I remember him telling me a little about it the last time we spoke.

'Yeah, it's going great, actually. I'm selling it. We're just working through the details now.'

'Wow, congratulations. That's amazing.'

'Yeah, it is. But it's also a little daunting. Technically, I'm going to be retired very soon, and I'm not sure how I feel about that.'

'I'm so jealous. I wish I could retire!'

Max seems to appreciate me reminding him that there are worse problems in the world than his, like being a waitress in a busy restaurant and being at least thirty years away from retirement myself. Of course, what he doesn't know is that I would love to seduce him and get with him more permanently, freeing me up to escape my dreary life and enjoy plenty of days in the sun with him instead.

'Well, if it's any consolation, you are excellent at your job.'

The compliment from Max fills my heart with pride and only makes me grow in confidence even more. I really do think he likes me, and now his wife isn't here, who knows what he might be willing to say to me?

'Hannah, Table Three needs clearing.'

Once again, Francesco has interrupted me.

'Of course,' I say, smiling at Max before telling him to enjoy his meal and rushing away.

I suppose I should be grateful that I wasn't disciplined by my manager in front of Max for attending to a table that is out of my jurisdiction, but I'm more annoyed that I can never get long enough with Max to really get anywhere with him. These brief moments of stolen conversation are not enough.

I'm going to have to see Max outside of this restaurant. I'm going to have to talk to him at home.

'Excuse me.'

I'm stopped on my way back to the kitchen, and I already know who it is before I look. It's Tom, or Tiresome Tom as I have started to think of him as.

'Yes, is everything okay with your meal?' I ask, just going into autopilot mode.

'My meal is fine. It's you I'm worried about.'

'Excuse me?'

'How long have you been in love with him?'

'What?'

'The gentleman at the table by the window. How long have you been in love with him?'

I realise that somehow, Tom has figured out that I am interested in Max. He must have gathered all of that simply by watching me. *God, am I that obvious?*

'Erm, I'm sorry, but I don't know what you're talking about,' I try, but it doesn't work because Tom is clearly too smart for that.

'It's okay. I'm not going to say anything to anyone else. But I have noticed, and I wanted to give you a word of warning.'

'You do?'

'Yes. I've seen the wedding ring on his finger, and I implore you not to get involved with a married man. It will not end well for any of the parties involved.'

'I'm sorry, but I really have to get back to work.'

But Tom doesn't let me go, actually grabbing hold of my arm as I try to walk away.

'I'm telling you. Don't do it. Leave him alone. You know it's for the best.'

I can see the sincerity in Tom's eyes, and it is almost as if he can see right into my soul and knows what I'm really thinking. But there's no way he can. To him, I must just seem like some foolish woman lusting after a married man. He won't know what I am really capable of and what I have done in the past because nobody knows. But he might find out in a moment if he doesn't let go of me.

'Is everything okay?'

This is the first time I've been grateful for my manager interrupting me tonight, and when he does, Tom removes his hand from my arm instantly.

I suppose I could make a scene here. Tell Francesco that this diner has been rude and behaved inappropriately. Have him removed from the restaurant. Make it known that he is not welcome here again.

But I don't do that. I just tell my boss that everything is fine and then walk away towards the kitchen, carrying on as if everything is normal. Maybe it can be.

So what if Tom knows I like Max? He's just some lonely guy who has a crush on me. I don't care about him. But one thing is for sure. If he ever touches me again, he won't have the manager to worry about.

He'll have me.

NADINE

I'm home alone but not for long. Kieran is on his way to my house, and a quick check on the time lets me know he should only be minutes away now. I told him to be here at eight o'clock, and that's not all I told him. I also assured him that my family would be in attendance this evening, and this would be the night when I told the truth about what happened in the past.

The fling. The pregnancy.

The lie over who the father was.

Kieran expects Adam to be here, as he expects Max to be here too. But neither are. They are both safely away. Adam's still at uni, and Max is at *San Bella*, where I sent him to dine alone after telling him that I was feeling unwell. I don't expect him to spend too long at the restaurant, considering he hasn't got anybody for company, but I won't need too long once Kieran gets here.

It won't take him long to realise that I have lied to him, but by then, it will be too late. He's been the one making ultimatums, but it's almost time for me to give him one. I hope he complies with my wishes, but if not, I have an insurance policy.

It's the knife tucked into the waistline of my jeans.

If Kieran continues to be a problem for me, I will have to become one for him.

The sound of the doorbell comes as a shock, even though I've spent the last hour expecting it.

Kieran is here.

And he's right on time.

When I was young, I had a way of dealing with daunting situations. I would take three deep breaths, just as my mother had advised me to do, before repeating the same word over and over again until I felt better. The word always changed, and it didn't really matter what it was. It just had to be something that emboldened me before I went into battle.

Back then, the things that worried me tended to be school exams or a performance in a play, and some of the words I used reflected the childish times. 'Elephant' was always a strong one because it was hard to be anxious when saying that word and filling my mind with the big-eared, long-nosed animal that seemed to connotate cuteness and peace. But as I've got older, the words have taken on more meaning, and right now, the word I feel like using is easily the one that makes me feel the most powerful.

Family.

I've taken my deep breaths, and now I'm saying that word over and over as I walk towards the front door and prepare to let Kieran into my home. As I'm saying it, images of Max, Adam and Sophie are flashing through my mind. Their smiling faces. Their silly ways. The memories we have shared together. And all the ones we still have to make.

By the time I reach the door, I'm feeling as strong as an ox. Nothing is going to stop me from getting my own way this evening. Kieran is on my territory now, and he is going to have to concede to my wishes. Not the other way around.

My way.

Or else.

Neither of us smiles at the other as I open the door, and we get a look at one another before the visitor breaks the silence.

'Are they here?'

'Yes.'

I step aside to allow him in, but to my dismay, he lingers on the doorstep for a second, looking around the driveway, and I'm wondering if he is trying to figure out if I am telling the truth.

Is everyone else inside?

Or am I lying to him?

I can feel the cool surface of the knife's blade against the skin of my lower back as I stand beside the open doorway and hope that he will come inside. It's mixed in with the cool air seeping into my warm house, and the longer I'm standing here, the more my temperature is dropping. But then Kieran makes his move, stepping into my home, and I'm glad he hasn't realised that something is wrong yet.

'So where are they?' he wants to know as I close the door.

I think about locking it, but I don't because that will only raise Kieran's suspicions, so it remains unbolted and still available as an escape route should either of us require it.

'In the kitchen. It's just this way.'

I lead Kieran towards the door at the other end of the hallway, aware that the silence in the house is not helping my claim that there are others inside with us. But

I only needed to get him inside. I can let him know the truth any second now.

I enter the kitchen and turn around to see Kieran as he walks in too, because it's at that point he realises I have been lying to him.

'Where is everybody?'

'I couldn't do it. I haven't told them.'

'You lying bitch! I should have known you wouldn't go through with this!'

'What do you expect? I'm not going to ruin my family for you.'

'You don't have a choice. I'm going to Adam right now, and if you stop me, I'll go to the police.'

Kieran turns back to leave, but I don't let him, rushing forward and grabbing his arm.

This is it. The moment of truth. My last shot at making him see things from my point of view and dropping all of this before it goes too far.

'Leave me and my family alone. I'm warning you.'

Kieran spins around, and for a second, I think he is going to strike me. But he doesn't, although he's clearly incensed.

'You've wasted my time with your stupid games!'

'You wasted mine. I was going to give you money. This could have been over by now.'

'Screw your money! And screw you! Enjoy your last night in your beautiful home. I'm sure your husband will have kicked you out by the morning once he's found out what you did.'

Kieran pulls his arm away, breaking free from my grip, and he is now heading towards the front door again.

This is it. The moment I realise I have no other choice. Not if I want to keep my family together.

I have to do this.

There is no other way.

I rush towards Kieran's back, pulling the knife from its hiding place as I go.

He doesn't turn around.

He doesn't know he's in danger.

He has no idea what's about to happen.

I plunge the knife into his lower back, surprised at how easily it slips through his clothing and his skin. I'm also surprised by the sound that Kieran makes as the weapon penetrates him. He lets out an awful, guttural moan as if he was full of air but is now deflating.

It's a noise that will stay with me for a long time. But the fact he is still making any sound tells me he isn't dead yet.

So I strike again. And again.

I stab him six times in total, which turns out to be the exact number I needed to get my victim to fall to the floor and curl up.

He's at my feet now. Defenceless. Bleeding. Whimpering.

I wonder if I will have to stab him one more time. Was that not already enough? I wait to find out. It's not as if he is going anywhere. He's too busy clutching his torso and gasping for air.

What vital organs did the knife puncture? The liver? The spleen? The kidneys? Or did I miss them all? Do the wounds look worse than they are? Am I going to have to change my area of attack, moving up from the torso to the head and neck area?

No. Whatever damage I caused, it is enough.

The blood keeps pouring, but Kieran has stopped moving.

My knife is no longer needed.

He's dead.

With shaking, bloodied hands, I take out my mobile phone and make a call.

'Help me! There's been an intruder! I stabbed him!'

I expect the person at the other end of the line to be shocked at first, before composing themselves and doing what is required of them. And to their credit, they do.

'Don't do anything. I'm on my way.'

I knew I could count on Max to come to my rescue. That's why I didn't call the police. This doesn't have to concern them. This could all be okay. I just want my husband to come home, and until then, I will do what I have always done.

Three deep breaths.

And then say a word that emboldens me.

HANNAH

I saw Max receiving a call on his mobile phone in the restaurant, but I couldn't hear what he was saying. All I did note was that whatever he heard at the other end of the line drained the colour from his face and caused him to get up from his table quickly. Now he's heading for the door, and Becki is chasing after him, no doubt wanting to make sure he pays for his meal before he departs.

But he doesn't seem to be slowing down.

It must be serious.

I decide to give Becki some assistance, although it's less out of duty as an employee here and more because I want to find out what is troubling Max.

'Is everything okay?' I ask as I reach the flustered man.

'You need to pay,' Becki says, stating the obvious, but she isn't helping, so I tell her that I will sort it out, and she seems relieved that it doesn't have to be her problem anymore.

Then I switch my attention to Max, who has set off towards the door again.

'Max? Excuse me. You need to tell me what's wrong, or they won't let you leave.'

I know it's only a matter of time until Francesco realises there is a customer threatening non-payment, and when he does, he will come over, and I'll lose whatever chance I have of finding out what Max's issue is.

'Max? Is everything okay?'

'No, it's not.'

His response is hurried, and it's clear he is a man with much bigger things on his mind than what might happen if he leaves a restaurant before settling his debt.

'What's happened?'

'It's my wife. I have to go.'

'Is she okay?'

'I don't know.'

I realise then that I'm not going to be able to stop Max. He is dead set on leaving, and I'm not strong enough to stop him, not that I would want to when he is like this. I don't think anyone would be wise to get in his way.

Enter my manager.

'Mr Murphy. Where are you going?'

Max doesn't slow down, and I can sense an argument coming here, so I intercept and do what I can to pacify my boss.

'Leave him. He has to go,' I say. 'Take it out of my wages.'

I make sure to say it loud enough for Max to hear me, and he does, turning back to look at me, no doubt surprised at my kind gesture in his hour of need. But Francesco isn't so thrilled by it. Quite rightly, he wants to know why I would want to do such a thing.

'He's got an emergency, but he'll pay me back,' I say. 'He's a loyal customer.'

'Yes, but-'

'-he has to go. Please. I'll sort it out. The restaurant won't lose any money.'

My plea seems to do the trick, and Francesco backs down, allowing Max to leave without any more hassle.

He doesn't thank me before he disappears through the front door, but that's okay. I'm sure he would have if he wasn't so stressed by whatever he heard on that call, and the main thing is that he knows I just helped him.

But now he is gone, I still need to know what was bothering him, and I won't be able to do that if I'm here.

'I'm really sorry, but I'm not feeling well. Would I be able to leave early?'

'What? It's Friday night!'

'I know, but we've got lots of staff on, and I never take sick leave. Please.'

My illustrious track record when it comes to illness and missed shifts plays in my favour, and I'm allowed to leave, clutching my stomach gingerly as I head for the staff exit to further sell my sudden bout of 'sickness.'

But I waste no time once I am out of view of Francesco, racing down the corridor and out towards the front of the restaurant where I see Max getting into his vehicle.

Searching for the lights of a vacant taxi in the vicinity of the *San Bella* car park, I see one driving past and flag it down as Max departs, turning right and speeding off. But I make sure my driver is going to be just as quick.

'Follow that car!' I tell the man at the wheel as I close the door and point at the vehicle in question through the windscreen.

The taxi driver doesn't question my wishes, which makes me wonder if this isn't the first time that he has had a passenger give him such an instruction. Then again, he probably doesn't care what his fares consist of as long as he gets them, and he puts his cab in motion without wasting any time.

We follow Max away from the restaurant and out of town, and my heart is racing as I keep my eyes on the taillights of his car up ahead. My mind is also racing with thoughts of what could be going on with him. He indicated that it was something to do with his wife.

Is Nadine okay? I'd have to guess not if he deemed it necessary to leave his meal and run for the door to be with her. But if she was ill or in trouble, then why not just call for an ambulance or the police? Max is certainly playing fast and loose with the speed limit right now, but I'm sure the emergency services could have still beat him home.

My taxi driver is unwilling to go quite as fast as the car we are trailing, but it's not a big problem if the gap between the vehicles widens a little. That's because we're out on the country roads now, and there is very little traffic around, meaning there's little chance of us losing Max, compared to if we were still in the town centre.

As the roads get darker and narrower, Max eventually slows down, and I instruct my driver to hit the brakes so we can observe from a distance. I want my presence to remain undetected, so it would do me no good to have the taxi pull up on Max's driveway, which is where I assume he is parking now. When I'm satisfied that Max has concluded his journey, I pay my driver what I owe him and step out onto the quiet country lane.

The cab leaves, and I creep towards the property that I saw Max park in front of, making sure to keep low and tucked into the side of the road where the hedges are. But Max has very little chance of spotting me due to the lack of light, and as I get closer to the house, I am confident I will remain unseen.

Peering around the side of a tree, I watch Max leave his car and run towards his front door, looking just as frantic as when I last saw him back at the restaurant. Then he goes inside and the door slams shut, putting me at a disadvantage as to know what happens next.

There's only one way for me to find out.

I'll have to get closer to the house.

It's time to discover what all the fuss is about.

NADINE

It's a relief to see my husband walk through the door. Now I'm not alone in this. There are two of us to fix this problem.

The problem that still resides by my feet.

Max's jaw hangs open when he sees Kieran's body on the floor, and it seems that telling him about it over the phone did little to dispel his shock when he sees it first-hand.

'Oh my God,' Max says as he stares at the corpse. 'What the hell happened?'

'I went outside to put something in the bin. He followed me in before I could get the door closed and told me he wanted money. I panicked and ran into the kitchen, and he chased me in. But he ran when he saw I had a knife.'

'You stabbed him?' Max asks as he surveys the bloody scene.

'Yes. I was scared! I thought he was going to hurt me!'

It's not hard to summon up a few tears after the events of tonight, and that only helps my cause in convincing Max that I am the victim here.

'Come here,' he says as he steps past the body and opens his arms to me. 'Did he touch you? Did he hurt you?'

'No, I'm okay.'

It feels good to be in Max's arms, and I wish I could stay pressed up against his chest all night. But we have the small matter of what to do next to talk about first.

'Should we call the police?' I ask him, purposely making it seem like we might have other options here. 'They'll believe me, won't they? They'll know it was just self-defence?'

'I don't know.'

'Oh my God. What if they arrest me? What they if they send me to prison for murder?'

'That's not going to happen.'

'How do you know that? It might. I killed him!'

I'm starting to panic, but I know it won't be long until my resourceful husband has an idea to improve our situation.

'Maybe we don't have to call the police,' he says a moment later, after my tears have soaked through his shirt.

'What do you mean?'

'We could hide the body. If no one knows he was here, then no one will come looking for him here.'

Does Max really mean that? He would hide a body for me?

'What if we get caught? We'll both go to prison. The kids…'

'We won't get caught. I'll take care of it.'

Max seems to slowly be coming out of the trance that he entered here in and is now moving into a much more productive state of mind.

'We need to move the body,' he tells me. 'We'll put it in my car, and I'll find somewhere to hide it.'

I feel physically sick as I think about Kieran being buried somewhere, potentially never to be found again. It's no way for a human being to leave this world. There should be a funeral. Loved ones mourning. A notice in the local newspaper. Something to mark the life that was lived. But this way, Kieran will just disappear.

A secret. A mystery.

A ghost.

But I also know that is the best thing for me, so I show that I am willing to help Max do whatever we need to do. It turns out that involves me lifting one end of the body while he manages the other, and as we pick Kieran up, I try not to look at all the blood that is still emanating from within him.

This hallway was always one of my favourite parts of this house due to how much light it gets and how good it looks to anybody entering the home. But now, I fear it will only ever remind me of the life I took and the amount of blood that was spilt on the hardwood floor.

It takes a lot of effort on both our parts, but Max and I manage to get Kieran out of the house and into the back of the car. It was hard not to imagine that there would be a load of police officers waiting on our driveway ready to pounce, just as soon as we stepped outside with a dead body between us, but that was not the reality. It's quiet up here. We're remote, and that means we are unseen.

Max is right.

We could get away with this.

It's a big relief to walk away from the body once it's safely stored in Max's vehicle, and once it is, he goes into the garage to get some tools that will help him bury it. I watch as he picks up a spade, a set of gardening gloves and a torch before he tells me that he is going to go because he's not sure how long it will take for him to dig a hole, and he doesn't want to waste time before sunrise. But he doesn't leave me without my own task to complete.

'Clean up in the hallway,' he tells me solemnly. 'Put everything into a bin bag. I'll burn it when I'm back.'

Max doesn't kiss me goodbye like he usually does before he gets in his car and leaves our house. Then again, it's not really the time for displays of affection and soppiness. It's a time for cold, calculated action, and he is doing what he needs to do, so I better get on with doing what I need to do.

I watch Max reversing out of the driveway, still feeling nauseous about what he is transporting. But I go in the house once he has left and get to work on scrubbing the hallway floor, filling up the mop bucket and not stopping until every drop of blood is gone.

It's tough work, but I can't help but feel like I got the easier end of the bargain. All I had to do was get on my hands and knees and clean. Poor Max is driving out to the middle of nowhere before having to dig a hole and drop Kieran's body into it. I suspect it will be hours before he is back.

Maybe I should have gone with him to make sure everything went okay. What if he gets stopped by the police and they discover what he has in the back of the car? What if he takes all the blame for my actions?

150

What if he spends the rest of his life in prison, even though I'm the one who sinned and not just the once?

I stop what I'm doing and try the deep breath technique again. But it's no good. It's not working this time. I simply have too much stress in my body, and nothing is going to calm me down until Max is back, and he tells me everything went as planned.

An hour has passed before I remember I am able to see the location of my husband's mobile on my phone. We shared each other's location for all the times he was away on business. He knows I like to see where he is, and he has said it comforts him whenever he checks on me and sees that I'm at home. But now I'm checking the app for a very different reason.

I want to see where my husband is burying the body I gave him.

It takes a while for the app to pinpoint his location, and I presume that's because he's out in the middle of nowhere, miles from a cell phone tower. But it eventually narrows in on one spot, and when it does, I see that Max is in the middle of Grove Forest. I had a feeling he might go there but seeing the little green dot in the middle of the wider green area on the map confirms it. That forest is huge, and in terms of finding a place to hide something within a twenty mile radius of our house, that would be the best bet.

I remember we took the kids to that forest once when they were little. Sophie and Adam ran around on the leaf-covered forest floor while Max and I walked behind them, hand in hand and smiling at their energetic ways. That seems a long time ago now. It was a long time ago. When things were innocent. But I guess they've never really been that innocent.

Not after what I did.

And now things are even worse. I'm a killer, and Max is a co-conspirator. Neither of us will ever be the same again. Will he eventually come to hate me for what I made him do for me? Will this drive a rift between us that we will never be able to bridge? Is this the beginning of the end for our marriage?

For everything?

Time will tell. It always does. Until then, I'll just have to keep telling myself that we will get away with this.

We won't get caught.

No one knows what we have done.

No one has seen us committing a crime.

HANNAH

That was easily one of the craziest nights of my life, and I've had some crazy ones in my time. I never thought I'd experience anything like the adrenaline rush I got when I killed Michael and Victoria two years ago but tonight has come close. That's because for the first time since then, I was in the presence of a dead body.

However, it wasn't me who did the killing this time. Based on what I can gather from what I saw, I think it was Nadine who was the murderer this evening. But Max isn't innocent in all of this. That's because I saw him putting the body in his car and driving off, presumably to get rid of the evidence.

Yep, it's been quite the night.

I'm home now after witnessing what I did in the darkness around the edges of the Murphys' home. But I doubt I'll be getting much sleep as I continue to keep pacing around this empty house and thinking back on what I saw.

I had been watching the Murphy house ever since Max went inside, but I had struggled to discern anything from a distance. That's why I went closer, in search of a window to see into the house through.

And boy, did I find one.

Of all the things I thought I might have seen when I peeped into the Murphys' hallway, the last thing I had expected was a butchered body. But there it was. Lying on the ground between Max and Nadine. Not moving. Blood everywhere. And a knife on the floor beside it that was obviously the murder weapon.

Nadine looked upset. Max looked shocked. But it explained why he had run away from *San Bella*. I imagine he didn't fancy hanging around to have a look at the dessert menu once he found out his wife had just taken a knife to some poor guy in their house.

I continued to watch as the couple embraced, and while it was a surprise to see Max being so supportive considering the crime his wife had clearly committed, it had also reinforced my belief that he was the man for me.

Loyal. Committed. *And brave.*

He displayed that bravery a few moments later when he had opened the front door before grabbing the arms belonging to the body and hauling it away. Nadine did her part in clearing up the mess by taking hold of the legs, and between them, the pair were able to get the corpse into their car.

I watched on from the side of the house as Max took several items from the garage before he got behind the wheel and started the engine. I was sad to see him go, but I hung back to watch what Nadine did next, and that was when I witnessed her scrubbing the blood from the hallway floor.

To be fair to her, she worked tirelessly until all the crimson colour was gone, and I imagine Max was having a harder time of it with his task. The thought of him out there cleaning up Nadine's mess made me angry, and I was very close to knocking on the front door and letting the woman inside know that I had seen everything and wanted her to pay for what she had done.

But cool heads prevailed, and I left the Murphy home without making my presence known, which I deemed to be for the best. This way, I have time to figure out my next move, and when I know what I want to do, I will get Nadine at a better time. In her state tonight, she most likely would have tried to kill me too if I had threatened her, so it's best to let things cool down a little before I speak to her and make her aware that she isn't quite the master criminal she thinks she is.

For now, I will wait, and I am doing that waiting while Max is out there somewhere digging a hole. My poor guy. I wish he knew I was thinking of him, and I also wish he knew that I would never make him do anything like this for me. Despite my past, I would not expect someone to cover up my crimes.

It makes me angry that Nadine is that way.

But she will pay for this. I just need to see to that.

The next couple of hours pass by slowly and painfully as I do nothing but lie on the carpet under my duvet and stare up at the ceiling. The moonlight filtering in through the window is giving the interior of this room a pale, whiteish hue, but despite that, all I can see is red. It's the after-effects of all that blood I saw tonight. I suffered the same thing after I killed the Spinners. It's as if the blood had soaked into my mind and disturbed my vision. I wonder if Nadine is experiencing the same thing. She could scrub the floor all she wants, but there's no removing that blood from her memory.

It's just after three am when I decide what I am going to do next. I will pay Nadine a visit when Max is

155

out of the house, and I will tell her that I saw everything. I will need to be careful, of course, because I know Mrs Murphy is not afraid to take desperate measures, but I am persuasive and have ways of keeping her calm.

I will make out like I can be a friend and can keep her crimes a secret, but only if she tells me why she killed that man. I want the truth, which may or may not be something she is willing to give me. Depending on what she says, I'll see where we can go from there.

But it's clear to me now that I am in a position of power. I want Max, and I will do anything to get him. With what I know and what I will learn in the future, that should only give me more of a chance of getting my man.

Nadine might have outsmarted that poor guy in her hallway.

But she won't outsmart me.

She's about to discover that I'm so much more than a waitress at her favourite restaurant.

NADINE

I've lost count of how many times I've mopped the hallway floor. It's been three days since I killed Kieran, but I still feel like his blood is everywhere in my home.

I see it on the floor. I see it on the walls.

And I see it in my dreams.

I have to hope that it will get easier. But I have no way of knowing that it will. I've never killed before. Maybe I'm now cursed to spend the rest of my life reliving the time I took someone else's.

The justification I had for what I planned to do seemed to make sense beforehand. Stopping Kieran to protect my family. It was a worthy motive. But now I've actually done it, I'm not so sure. Yes, I've kept my family together but at what price? I must carry this terrible burden now, as must Max, the man who helped hide the body.

My husband was painfully quiet when he got home after his trip out into Grove Forest. It was almost dawn when he got back, and I had been sitting by the window waiting for him to return. The first hint of sunlight was cresting on the horizon, but there was no mistaking the darkness on my man's face as he got out of his car and made his way to our garage, carrying the tools he had used to dig the grave that we both hope will never be found.

I had gone outside to meet him, but he didn't say a word to me as he had put away the dirty spade and the soil-soaked gloves before heading for the house. It was at that point that I grabbed his hand to make him stop and talk to me. I wanted to make sure that he was alright, but really, I just wanted him to tell me that I was going to be alright. In the end, neither happened. He just said two simple words and walked away.

'It's done.'

We haven't spoken about it since. I tried to broach the subject a couple of times, but Max cut me off straight away. It's clear he has chosen to deal with the guilt by stuffing it down deep inside and never letting it out.

He's on the road again now, attending meetings and somehow still finding the mental capacity to work on the sale of his business. As for me, I've been cooped up in the house ever since that fateful night, and I still don't feel like going out anytime soon. I've stopped short of drawing the curtains during daylight hours, but I am having a hard time functioning properly. I've got so many text messages from friends to reply to, so many errands to run, and I really need to get some exercise, but all I can seem to muster the energy for is making a cup of tea and sitting on the sofa before staring into space.

I need something to snap me out of this funk.

And then I get it.

The sound of the doorbell forces me to have to go into the hallway to reach the front door, and once there, I'm hit by flashbacks of Kieran as he reacted to the knife entering his body. The fear that it could be the police calling to ask me questions is very real, but I tell myself it's not them. But if it is, then choosing not to answer the door won't make a difference anyway. I'm sure they would just barge in if they really thought I was a murder suspect.

But there are no police officers on my doorstep. There's just a woman I know from somewhere.

It's the waitress from *San Bella.*

Hannah, was it?

What the hell is she doing here?

'Hi, Mrs Murphy. I was wondering if I could come in?'

I'm racking my brains for any reason why this woman would need to come into my house and talk to me. The only thing I can think of is that there might have been a problem with the payment going through for one of our many meals at *San Bella.* But that's unlikely, and even then, wouldn't the staff just call? The phone number is logged with our reservations.

But not our address.

'How do you know where I live?' I want to know, feeling my anxiety starting to rachet up. I almost suspect everyone of knowing my shameful secret now, even though there is no reason they should. It's like I still have Kieran's blood on my hands, and it's obvious to anyone who looks at me.

'I think it will be easier if you just let me in, and then we can talk properly,' Hannah replies very calmly. But it's still not good enough.

'What are you doing here?'

'Calm down. I come in peace. But you don't want to turn me away. Trust me on that.'

Hannah's tone of voice makes me feel like I have no other choice. I do trust her that it would be best to let her in, even though I don't know why. Whatever she wants to say, it's something I have to hear.

I step aside and allow her in, still silently praying that this won't have anything to do with something that could cause me a problem. But the odds of that are dwindling by the second.

'You have a lovely home,' Hannah says as she looks around the hallway and I close the door. 'It's beautiful.'

'Thank you. I'm sorry, but I'm still a little confused. What is it you want?'

I watch Hannah as she seems to be examining the place. But she's not looking at the artwork on the walls or the architecture of the staircase. Instead, she is looking down at the floor.

At the exact place where Kieran lay dying.

'I saw what you did,' Hannah tells me, breaking the unbearable silence but saying the one thing that was worse than nothing at all.

'What?'

'You killed that man right here. Stabbed him. This is where he was.'

She gestures with her right hand to the area between us, pointing out what I already know.

This is where the body was.

But I can't just concede so easily. I have to try and deny this, even though it's true.

'I don't know what you mean.'

'Oh, come off it. I saw everything. Okay, so I missed the part where you killed that guy, but I saw him

160

on the floor here. And I saw you and your husband put the body in the car.'

Oh my God, she really does know everything.

My legs have gone all wobbly, and I stumble backwards a little, reaching out for the wall to make sure I don't completely tumble over. This can't be happening. How is this possible?

'How?' is all I can muster as I stare at the calm, composed waitress in my home.

'I saw Max leaving the restaurant in a hurry. He looked stressed, and when I asked him if everything was okay, he said it was something to do with you. He left without paying, so I knew it was serious. So I got out of my shift early and followed him.'

'You followed my husband? Why would you do that?'

'I wanted to make sure everything was okay.'

'Why would you care?'

That's when Hannah displays the first signs of annoyance at me and my questions. She didn't seem bothered when I was playing dumb about the body, but she does seem bothered now I've expressed confusion as to why she should care about me or my husband.

'I've been watching you both, ever since you've been coming to *San Bella*,' she tells me. 'It was hard not to be drawn to the two of you. You look so good together. The perfect couple. Or so I thought.'

'You're stalking us?'

'No, it's not stalking if you came to my workplace. But I'll admit that I did spend a lot of time observing you both. What you were wearing. What you

161

ordered. Whether you seemed happy or sad. Chatty or quiet. You brightened up my dull shifts, that's for sure.'

'Why?'

'I suppose I envied you.'

'Me?'

'Yeah. You got to go out for dinner every Friday night with a handsome man, while I was stuck serving tables in a stupid uniform. I'm sure you wouldn't have wanted to swap places with me, would you?'

I don't answer that or make any movement that would indicate she is correct with that assumption. But Hannah takes that as agreement anyway.

'I was jealous. But that was all. I might have left things there, but then I saw Max leaving, and I wanted to know what was going on. Perhaps the perfect couple weren't so perfect after all. That's why I followed him. And that's how I saw what the pair of you did.'

'So what is this? You're here to blackmail us?'

'I didn't use that word.'

'No, but I did. Is this what all this is about? Do you want money?'

'You'd like that, wouldn't you? I'm sure it would be very easy for you in your big home to pay off some silly waitress who needs the cash.'

'Just tell me what you want!'

'I want the truth. Why did you kill that man?'

The truth that Hannah is seeking is one that I have already killed for to keep quiet before, so there can be no way I will tell her, even with what she knows.

'He broke in. It was self-defence.'

'You must think I was born yesterday.'

'That's what happened. I swear!'

'You think the police would buy that? Because I don't. If it was self-defence, then you could have just called them. They'd want to know why you hid the body. That makes it more suspicious.'

'I was scared. I panicked. And Max just wanted to protect me!'

'Oh, so it's Max's fault now, is it? You're really blaming this on your husband, who, as far as I can tell, did not kill anybody and was just helping you, the real criminal here?'

I get the sense now that Hannah likes Max a lot more than me, so I need to remember that with how I talk to her going forward.

'Okay, you saw what happened. I get it. And I'm sorry for what I did. But what do you want me to do about it?'

'I told you. I want you to tell me why you killed him. And be careful because I want the truth this time, or I will have to take this to the police.'

Hannah takes out her mobile from her pocket then and waves it at me.

'What's that?'

'I didn't just look through the window the other night. I filmed what I saw too.'

My legs are getting weaker by the second, and I want to sit down, but I have to stay standing, and I have to stay strong here in the face of such adversity.

'Why would you do that? Why would you ruin us?'

'I'd ruin you.'

'And Max! He'd go to prison for this too. Would you want that?'

I'm testing to see how much Hannah really cares about my husband, and as I suspect, she fails that test.

'This was not his fault. It was yours.'

'We're in this together.'

Hannah doesn't seem to like me saying that, but there's not much she can do about it because it is the truth. It seems that is forcing her to recalibrate, and she takes a moment to figure out her next move.

'Do you think you deserve your husband?'

'Excuse me?'

'Deep down, do you think you deserve him?'

'Yes, I do.'

'Then prove it. Tell me the truth about why you killed that man, or you will both go to prison.'

I can see that Hannah is serious. There's a sort of vengeful air to her, like she is not just doing this because it's the right thing to do but because she is almost mad at me, at Max maybe, and possibly about how her own life has turned out. But that makes her dangerous and unpredictable.

I might have to do this.

I might have to finally share my secret with someone.

'He wasn't an intruder,' I begin with my voice shaking. 'I knew him.'

'Who was he?'

'We slept together, many years ago.'

'An ex?'

'Not exactly.'

164

It takes Hannah a moment before she gets it.

'You had an affair?'

'It was a long time ago.'

The look on Hannah's face is making me regret going down this path because she looks incredulous. But perhaps a few lies can make her sympathise with me.

'I made a mistake. I know that. But I didn't deserve what happened next. Kieran got violent with me. That was his name, the man I killed. He was dangerous, and I got away from him, but he found me all these years later. Broke in while Max was out. Said he's been watching me for a while. And he threatened me. I thought he was going to kill me. So I killed him first.'

I'm praying that Hannah buys my story without me really having to tell the truth and bring Adam into this, and it's a relief when that seems to be the case.

'I'm sorry you were in danger,' she says quietly. 'But you brought it on yourself when you had the affair.'

'I've regretted it every day since.'

'I'm sure you have, but it doesn't change what you did.'

'I know, but I can't change the past! No one can! So what do you want me to do?'

'I want you to leave Max.'

'What?'

'You heard me. Leave your husband, and all of this goes away.'

'No, I'm not leaving him. I love him!'

'You have a funny way of showing it.'

'How dare you!'

But it seems Hannah isn't finished yet.

'I lost everything because my partner cheated on me. So you have to lose it all too. You're not the victim here, Max is. He deserves the truth, and he deserves to be with someone who loves him and would never hurt him. Someone like me.'

So that's what this is all about. I see it now. Hannah is in love with Max. That's why she was watching us at the restaurant. That's why she followed him when he left suddenly. And that's why she is here. She doesn't give a damn about the truth or justice for Kieran. She just wants me out of the picture so she can have my man all to herself.

But that's not going to happen.

'You're pathetic. You really think I'm just going to let you take my husband.'

'I do if it means you get to stay out of prison.'

'So you are blackmailing me.'

'I just want the best for Max. And I don't think you are it.'

It's time to call this woman's bluff.

'Fine, go to the police,' I say defiantly. 'Show them the video and tell them everything. But you'll lose Max. He'll be in a cell, and you'll be out here, still as lonely as you are now.'

'Don't push me.'

'Don't push me either. Not now you know what I'm capable of.'

'I'll give you a few days to think about it. Allow you to see sense. But if you don't leave Max, then I will ruin you.'

Hannah walks towards the door, and a big part of me wants to reach out and grab her by the hair and drag her into the kitchen, where I know the other knives are. But another part of me senses that I won't be able to trick her like I tricked Kieran. He wasn't worried about turning his back on me because he had no idea what I was willing to do. But Hannah knows, and she makes sure to keep her distance and her eyes on me as she gets to the door.

'You can let me know on Friday night when you come to the restaurant if you like,' Hannah says after opening the door and allowing some fresh air into this very stuffy house. 'I'll let you enjoy one last meal with your husband before you walk away, if that's what you need.'

With that, Hannah leaves, and I'm left watching her go, mostly hating her but also a little in awe at her confidence to come here and be this way with me.

She thinks she has already won.

But she better think again.

HANNAH

I strolled into the restaurant tonight feeling like a winner, and that must explain why I've been in such a good mood with everyone I've crossed paths with, including my colleagues here, the diners and the takeaway driver who came in to collect a dish from the kitchen. I've greeted them all with a warm and wide smile, and even if it wasn't reciprocated, I haven't let it knock me off my stride.

The reason for my euphoric mood this evening is because I feel like my little 'chat' with Nadine went well and that with my threats made, there is no way she won't back down and let me get closer to what I want.

I'm feeling so good that I'm even chatty with Becki, my much younger colleague who I usually can't stand the sight of. The feeling is always mutual, but tonight, I'm chirping away at her like we are two long-lost besties.

'What have you got planned this weekend? Anything fun?'

Becki frowns when she hears my questions before looking around to see if I was directing it at somebody else. But then she realises I was talking to her and just looks confused.

'Why do you ask?'

'Just wondering. I would have thought there would be lots of exciting things going on at your age.'

'Erm, yeah, I guess.'

'Like what? A nightclub on Saturday night? Or a house party, perhaps?'

Becki is not warming up to me at all, but it doesn't matter because nothing can take the wind out of my sails, and as I breeze back onto the restaurant floor, I'm not even perturbed by the sight of Tom sitting at one of the tables.

It seems my admirer is back and while that irritated me on other nights, I think now is a good time to be nice to him and not let his over-eagerness bother me.

'Hi, how's your meal going?' I ask him.

Tom seems surprised to see me, or maybe it's just that I'm being nice instead of dismissive. Either way, he smiles and tells me his meal is going well so far.

'Great. Glad to hear it. I know I'm not your waitress this evening, but if there's anything you need, don't hesitate to give me a shout.'

I expect Tom to thank me and perhaps ask for another drink but he doesn't. Instead, he just looks suspicious.

'Why are you being so nice to me?'

'Excuse me?'

'Is it because you feel bad for turning down my offer of a drink before?'

'What? No, of course not.'

'So you don't feel bad?'

'I'm just being friendly.'

'I see. Because you want a tip?'

'No, because it's just nice to be nice.'

I'm starting to wish I hadn't bothered now, but I'm stuck here until Tom lets me go.

'Have you changed your mind about going on a date with me?'

Oh God, I really wish I hadn't bothered talking to him now.

'Erm, no. I'm sorry.'

Tom looks crestfallen at that, and I wonder if I have been too harsh, so I end up saying something I'll probably regret later.

'How about I think about it,' I say, giving him some encouragement that he might not need.

'Really? Great!'

It seems I've just made his day, or maybe it's his month, but whatever: the customer is happy, and that's all that matters. I'm sure he'll forget all about this conversation eventually. I know I will.

It feels like it's my job to spread happiness and joy around *San Bella* this evening, and after pleasing Tom, I compliment a young girl on her pretty dress and also offer to take a photo of a couple who look like they are celebrating a birthday. Then it's back into the kitchen I go, and when I get there, I hear the news circulating amongst the staff that the new rota is complete and available for us to check.

Joining the small crowd that has gathered around the A4 piece of paper that has been stuck to the wall, I scan the list of names for my own before checking to see which days I am due to be on duty. I'm not expecting much to have changed because I always get given the same shifts and never ask to alter them, but it's sensible to check anyway to avoid any problems.

But then I notice that I do have a problem.

There has been a change in my regular shift pattern.

170

I'm not due to be working this Friday night.

'Hey, why am I not working Friday?' I ask out loud to no one in particular as I double-check the rota.

'Why are you complaining?' Becki replies, and one of the chefs sniggers. But I'm not laughing. I'm complaining. That's because I want to work Friday. I want to be here when the Murphys come in because that's when Nadine is supposed to tell me what she is going to do.

I take my query to Francesco, demanding to know why my shifts have been changed unexpectedly, before asking to be reinstated to Friday night. But he tells me he won't alter the rota and that he didn't think it would be a problem.

'Enjoy a Friday night off for a change. You've earnt it.'

But that's not good enough for me, and after failing to get him to see things my way, I decide to try and get one of the other waitresses to swap their shifts with me. I'm counting on someone like Becki jumping at the chance to get out of work and enjoy a Friday night. But to my surprise, she doesn't take that chance. She just tells me that she needs the money and won't swap her shift, as does every other waitress here. One of them even calls me "sad" for trying to get reinstated to Fridays, but I just shoot her a death stare before leaving the kitchen, confused and annoyed.

This is not convenient.

I'm going to have to figure out another way of seeing the Murphys on Friday now.

But how?

NADINE

It's sometimes difficult to make contact with my husband when he is away on business. The number of meetings he goes into means his phone is often switched off, and because he's always on the move, it's not as if I can just contact his secretary at the office and get her to interrupt him. But if ever there was a time when I needed to speak to him, then it's now. After Hannah's visit and the bombshell that somebody saw what we did that night Kieran died, I have to let Max know, and then we both have to make a plan to get ourselves out of this mess.

This could go a number of ways, but one way it will not end will be with Hannah getting my husband, like she wants.

Over my dead body.

Or, more preferably, over hers.

I've left voicemails and sent several texts to Max's phone, so I know he will be in touch as soon as he turns his mobile on and sees how desperate I am to speak with him. I've not been so stupid as to put anything incriminating in the messages, aware that even with the best planning and best of luck, we could be investigated by the police one day. If that happens, then I'd hate for them to have the crucial bit of evidence they need in the form of me saying to Max that 'somebody saw us move the body.' I just said there was a problem at home and left it at that. No detective could say that has anything to do with a potential murder.

I've tried several things to calm my nerves while waiting for Max to call. I've run on our treadmill, I've showered, and I've made myself a sandwich. I've also drunk a couple of glasses of wine when all that earlier stuff failed to work. But I'm still a nervous wreck, and I will be until Max tells me how everything is going to be okay.

It's almost ten o'clock at night when I see my husband trying to get in touch via a video call. I can't connect the call quickly enough, and it's a relief to see Max's face flash up on my phone's screen. He looks tired, and the tie around his shirt collar is hanging loose, a sign that he is finished with business for the day but is too weary to get changed into more comfortable clothing.

'Hey, I've seen all the messages. Is everything okay? I've been stuck in a meeting all day.'

'No, everything's not okay. We've got a big problem.'

'What?'

'Somebody saw what we did.'

'What do you mean?'

'The body, Max! Somebody saw the body!'

I see my husband's eyebrows rise as the seriousness of this dawns on him, but then he frowns, his overworked mind trying to now work out another problem before he gets to rest it during sleep.

'Who?'

'The damn waitress from *San Bella*. She followed you home after you ran out of the restaurant. She saw everything.'

'What waitress?'

174

'Hannah! She's obsessed with us! Or rather, she's obsessed with you!'

'What the hell are you talking about?'

I sigh before running Max through everything that I discussed with that crazy waitress, including how she wants him and will only keep our secret quiet if I give him to her.

'This is insane,' is his best offering when I've finished, and while that is true, it's not much help.

'What are we going to do about it?' I want to know, staring at the confused face on my phone.

'I'll have to talk to her.'

'I don't want you going anywhere near her. She's in love with you. Who knows what she'll do!'

'Don't be ridiculous. She isn't in love with me.'

'You didn't hear her. She was serious. She is obsessed. She's been watching us every Friday night. All this time. God, why didn't we just go to a different restaurant? Why did we keep going back there every week?'

'Because you like it there!'

'Don't blame this on me!'

'I'm not blaming it on anybody. I'm just trying to figure it out.'

'What's there to figure out? She says we have to give her our answer on Friday night when we're next at *San Bella*. But we can't give her what she wants, can we? So what other choice do we have?'

Max takes a moment to think about it as I feel like I'm losing myself to the anger swelling up inside of me. All I want to do is march down to that damn Italian restaurant, drag Hannah out by her hair and throw her in the same hole Kieran got put into. It might not be the wisest thing to do, but it would certainly satisfy my soul tonight.

Thankfully, my husband has another idea.

'What if we offered her money?'

'What?'

'We could try and pay her off. Give her cash for keeping quiet. She's a waitress, she must need the money.'

'I don't think that'll work. I already tried it. She didn't want money.'

'Maybe she doesn't know how much we could give her. It'd be enough for her to never have to work in that restaurant again, that's for sure.'

'I don't know,' I say, but it's not just because I'm doubting if it could work. It's because I'm unsure how happy I feel about potentially making a very wealthy woman out of the person who came into my home and threatened me. In my view, Hannah doesn't deserve to be paid off for spying on us and telling me she wants my man.

'I'll make her an offer on Friday night,' Max tells me. 'Try and make her see sense. She'd be mad not to go for it.'

'Oh, she's mad, alright. There's no doubt about that.'

'Maybe she'll be calmer if it's coming from me. If she likes me as much as you say she does, then I must have a chance of talking her into not making this any worse. And besides, we'll be in a public place. There's not much she will be able to do at *San Bella*.'

'You're talking like she is some level-headed person. But she isn't. She's lost her mind. All that time, we thought she was just being a good hostess, and in reality, she was watching our every move and dreaming up silly fantasies in her head about you and her being together.'

'I get that, but we have to try and meet her halfway. We're not exactly innocent here, are we? So we can't act like we are.'

'Yes, I know that! I didn't say we were!'

'Let's not get into a fight. I'm so close to making the sale now, and then we'll have everything we ever wanted. We can still make this work. We just need to stay calm and stick together.'

I know Max is right. This might feel like the end of the world, but it might not have to be. If I can deal with Kieran, I can deal with Hannah.

Hopefully, she'll take the offer of money, and then it will be over.

If not, I really hope Max has a good Plan B.

HANNAH

I came up with a clever way of getting around my problem of not being on shift at *San Bella* on Friday night. I realised that if I couldn't be there as an employee, then I would just have to be there as a paying customer instead. That's why I decided to book myself a table at 19:15, and I made sure to ask for Table Seven because I know that is the closest one to Table Six, where the Murphys will be sitting.

There was some surprise on the part of my colleagues when they found out I was choosing to spend my Friday night off at my workplace, but I don't care about their opinions. They've always been small-minded to me, and they have never been able to see the bigger picture. To them, I'm just a lonely, boring woman who seems to lack the ambition or skillset to progress beyond my line of work. But that's not who I am. I'm actually a very smart and very driven person, and I'm hoping that after tonight, I will also get the exact thing I've wanted for most of my shifts at *San Bella*.

Not a pay rise or a promotion.

A person.

It's Becki who has the privilege of being my waitress this evening, and she looks at me like I'm a lunatic as she leads me to my table.

'Why are you here?' she wants to know. 'I can't believe you'd want to pay to be at work.'

'I'll start with an Espresso Martini, thank you,' I say, not letting her forget who is in charge here. They say the customer is always right, and tonight, Becki will have to respect me, whether she likes it or not.

As I watch the young waitress go over to the bar to place my drink order, I glance across at the table beside me. The napkins are folded and sitting on the small plates beside the two place settings. The wine glasses are sparkling and just waiting to be filled with something from a vintage year in the vineyards of Southern France. And the chairs are tucked in, currently unoccupied but very soon to be warmed by the behinds of my very favourite couple.

I made sure to book my reservation a little earlier than theirs because I wanted to be comfortable when they arrived. I also wanted to make sure I caught them off guard. The Murphys will be expecting to see me in uniform, so they'll be on the back foot when they spot me sipping a cocktail at the table next to them.

'Thank you,' I say to Becki after she has reluctantly brought me my beverage, but I send her on her way again a moment later by telling her that I need a little more time to peruse the food options. She frowned again when I said that, probably because she must know that I could recite every item on this menu by heart if I had to, but why should I rush? I'm paying for a Friday night out, and I'll take as long as I want to take.

I'm halfway through my cocktail when the hands on my watch tell me it's seven-thirty. But the table beside me is still empty. Are the Murphys going to show? How can they not? The risk would be too great for them to defy me.

Becki comes back to my table again to take my food order, but I tell her I'd like one more cocktail first. She rolls her eyes before walking away, and that little gesture has almost certainly confirmed in my mind that I won't be leaving a tip when I'm done. I was going to give her ten pounds, even if I can't really afford it, but not anymore. That's what she gets for treating me with disdain.

One person who has never treated me that way is the man I can see across the restaurant when I turn around to look behind me. Tom is here by himself again, as he often is, and he gives me a wave when he sees me looking. But I don't return the gesture because I don't want him to think that he might have a chance at coming to join me at my table.

I'd like to keep him over there, out of the way, and while I'm sure he'll be watching me, he won't be able to hear me.

'Here you go. Your usual table. May I take your coats?'

I turn back around when I hear the sound of Francesco's voice and when I do, I see that he has led Max and Nadine to the table next to me. But both of them have ignored the question and are just staring at me, clearly surprised to see that I am off-duty this evening.

I wait for them to be seated and their coats and jackets taken to the cloakroom before I speak, and by the time I do, Becki has furnished me with my second drink, giving me the chance to raise my glass to Max and welcome him once again to *San Bella*.

'Nice night for some good food, don't you agree?' I ask, but neither Max nor Nadine answer me. They also don't seem to be showing much interest in looking at the menu. With that in mind, I suppose it would be best to get the business out of the way before the food.

'So, have you considered my offer?' I ask as I run my finger around the rim of my martini glass.

'We have a counter-offer,' Max replies, piquing my interest.

'And what would that be?'

'We'll give you a quarter of a million pounds to leave us alone. Cash, if you want it that way. And you can have it tonight.'

Max studies me for my reaction, but it's Nadine who I am interested in. But she isn't even looking at me, and that makes me think that the money was not her idea.

'This isn't what your wife and I discussed,' I say to Max. 'Did she tell you what I really want?'

I keep running my finger around the edge of my glass, a part of me hoping that it might look a little seductive to the man at the next table. His eyes do follow my finger a few times, but he mainly does a good job of keeping his gaze on my face.

What does he think of the effort I've made? The dress? The heels? The hair? I look a hell of a lot better than I do in my uniform, and I wonder if seeing me this way might be making Max reconsider.

'Yes, she told me,' he confirms. 'But I'm afraid that's out of the question.'

'And why is that?'

'Because I love my wife, and I won't leave her.'

'You love her even though she killed a man?'

'Keep your voice down. He was an intruder.'

'Was he?'

That's when Nadine brings herself to look at me, no doubt afraid that I'm about to let Max know that she actually knew the man she murdered. But I won't divulge that information yet. It will be good to keep it in reserve, for if and when I really do need it.

'He broke in and threatened her. It was self-defence,' Max assures me, and I wonder if he would be able to be so calm and convincing if he was talking to a policeman.

'Okay, that's not important right now,' I say, batting the air. 'What is important is that I have told you what I want, and that is all I want. I'm not interested in your money. I only want you, Max.'

'But he doesn't want you!' Nadine snarls, looking like she enjoyed that.

'Nadine, please,' Max says, obviously reminding her to stay calm, and I figure that was something they discussed on their way here this evening. Then the man of the table speaks to me again.

'Half a million.'

The offer is going up, and while it's not surprising to me, it is clearly bothering Nadine. But Max is a big boy, and he must know what he is doing.

'I've told you. I don't want your money.'

'Why not? You could start a new life with it. Get away from this place. Do whatever you want to do.'

182

'Money doesn't make me happy. Being in love does that. And I'm in love with you, Max. Can't you see that?'

'But I'm married! Can't you see that?'

He flashes his wedding ring at me as if I'd never caught sight of it before. But it'll take more than that to put me off.

'I appreciate that we've got to know each other under strange circumstances. But I am willing to bet that if things were different and we actually spent time together, you could learn to love me even more than your wife.'

'Get your own man!' Nadine cries a little too loudly for the people at the tables around us not to hear.

'I had my own man. But he left me. It's just how things go. True love is a lie. In reality, people just take what they want. So that's what I'm doing here.'

'I knew this was a waste of time,' Nadine says, and she looks like she is ready to leave, barely five minutes after she got here. 'I told you she was crazy.'

Nadine's insult washes over me harmlessly because it's only Max's opinion that I care about here. Could he love me? Could he leave his wife for me? Could he give me what I want in order to avoid losing everything?

'A million. That's as high as I can go,' he says, showing me he is still on a completely different page to the one I'm on.

'Max! What are you doing?' Nadine cries. 'We're not giving her that much!'

She isn't happy about it either, and at least we agree on something.

'Do I have to remind you that I could ruin you both with one simple phone call to the police?' I say calmly as the restaurant hums around us, and the waitresses have no idea their colleague is engaged in such a serious conversation between Tables Six and Seven.

'But what would you gain from telling the police about us?' Max wants to know. 'They'd ask why you didn't come forward sooner, and then we'd tell them about the blackmail. You'd be in almost as much trouble as us then.'

Nadine smirks at me, assuming that her husband has just scored a point for them. But that's not what's happened, and I'm about to let them know it.

'I'm a single waitress with no life outside of these four walls, so I'm prepared to lose everything to potentially gain something. But are you?'

I've made my stance clear. I don't give a damn about getting in trouble with the police. But I know the Murphys do.

'If you keep threatening us, then I swear to God I'll make you wish you'd never been born,' Nadine hisses at me as she gets out of her seat and looks like she might go for me. But Max skilfully intervenes, and after telling his wife to wait outside, she leaves the pair of us alone.

Then Max takes a seat in the chair opposite me, and I wonder if this might be the moment when I get what I want.

It's not. But what I do get isn't so bad.

'Where do you live?' Max wants to know. 'I think it's better if we talk somewhere more private. Just the two of us.'

'No Nadine?'

'No Nadine.'

I like the sound of that, so I request Max's number and tell him I will send him my address, or at least the address I am secretly staying at. I suspect my time is running out in terms of how long I can get away with living in the Spinner residence, so I might as well see if I can get Max there before I leave it behind for good.

'I'll come by later tonight. When my wife's asleep,' he tells me as he gets up from the table.

'I look forward to it,' I tell him with a mischievous smile.

He doesn't return the expression. All he does is apologise to Becki and say that he and his wife have to cancel their booking. She looks confused. He looks harassed. And Nadine is already gone.

But I'm happy.

I've got a cocktail in my hand.

I've also got a date with Max later tonight.

NADINE

I'm pacing around in the restaurant car park when Max finally appears after staying back to say something to Hannah. I demand to know what was said after I'd left, but he only tells me once we are in the car on our way home. He pretends that's because it's cold out, but I know it's just so he can get me away from *San Bella* before Hannah and I can cross paths again.

'I've told her to reconsider my offer,' Max tells me. 'Sleep on it. See what she thinks in the morning.'

'She won't change her mind. She's too stubborn.'

'Let's give her one more chance.'

'No, let's not! Every minute we leave this unresolved is another minute when she could go to the police!'

'She won't go to the police. She's not as stupid as you think.'

'How do you know? We barely know anything about this woman. This time last week, we thought she was just a friendly waitress who was good at serving us our drinks. Now we know she is dangerous.'

'We have to stay calm.'

'I can't stay calm. Not with this hanging over us. We have to do something.'

'Like what?'

'We have to end this. Get rid of her. We could do it. We've got away with it once. What do you say?'

Max hits the brakes then, and my seatbelt is the only thing that stops me from going into the dashboard.

'What are you doing?' I cry as I try and relieve the pressure of the fabric across my chest.

'What am I doing? What are you doing? Are you seriously saying we should try and get away with hiding a second body? Because if you are, then I'd say it's not Hannah who's the crazy one. It's you!'

'We can't reason with this woman! She won't even take a million pounds!'

'We can't kill her. I won't do that. The first time was an accident. This would be real murder, with a motive, and that's very different to killing an intruder. If that's who they were.'

'What do you mean by that?'

'Why did Hannah seem to suggest that there was more to it than that?'

I was hoping that Max would have missed that but sadly not.

'I don't know. She'll say anything to get her way.'

'Will she?'

'Yes!'

I don't believe this. Is Max actually starting to have some sympathy with this woman, and even worse, could he start believing her over me?

'This has to stop. Before it gets any worse for us. I say we ask her to come to our house and pretend like we're going to give her what she wants. But then we kill her. It's the only way to make sure our secret stays safe.'

'I refuse to believe that murder is the only way.'

'But what if it is?'

Max doesn't answer that for a while, and we sit in silence in our car that is just sitting in the middle of the road where my husband deemed it fit to slam on the brakes.

'We need to move,' I remind him, checking in the rearview mirror to make sure there are no vehicles approaching us from behind, and that stirs him into action.

We spend the rest of the journey saying very little. I've made my case, and it seems he has made his, but so far, we haven't got anywhere.

I make us some food when we get in. I'd already been anticipating I might have to cook because I had a feeling our night at *San Bella* would not go well. But Max barely touches the cheap supermarket pizza I give him, and I don't get more than halfway through my own before I decide to call it a night.

Max is clearly trying to distract himself from the bigger problems at hand because he asks me if I have seen his gym card and then spends ten minutes looking around the house for it. I don't know why he's bothered because he never actually goes to the gym, but I guess the search takes his mind off things. But it proves to be fruitless, and he gives up, muttering something about how his cards are always falling out of his wallet.

'What are we going to do about her?' I ask Max as we both get into bed and turn off the lights.

'I'll decide in the morning,' he tells me, and then he rolls over without giving me a kiss, making me fear that I'm the one annoying him the most right now and not Hannah, the psycho stalker.

I go seeking some reassurance from him by snuggling up alongside him and putting my arm over his waist before giving his shoulder a small kiss. He doesn't tell me to leave him alone, which is good, but he doesn't exactly warm to my touch either, and closing the distance between us physically hasn't quite done the job emotionally.

'I'm so sorry about all of this,' I tell him in a whisper. 'This is all my fault. I shouldn't have killed that man. If I had just let him do whatever he wanted to do, then I would have been the victim here, and Hannah wouldn't have anything on us.'

I'm hoping my play for a little sympathy is going to do the trick in making Max feel bad for me again, and it does when I feel him rolling over to face me in the bed.

'Don't be silly. I'm glad you fought back. I'm glad you defended yourself and our home.'

'I know, but this wouldn't be happening if I had just left it. I feel so bad for making you bury that body. I can't imagine what you went through in those woods.'

Max doesn't say anything to that, and it feels like the weight of the silence is proof enough that he harbours memories from his trip into the woods that he will never be able to forget.

'Let's just go to sleep, and we'll decide what to do in the morning,' he tells me, repeating what he said as we got into bed a short while ago. Then he gives me a kiss, which goes some way to helping me relax enough to try and get some sleep this evening. Sure enough, I eventually drift off about an hour after we turned out the lights, and when I sleep, I dream of nothing.

Nothing good. Nothing bad. Just the black, inky darkness of my mind preparing itself for another busy day tomorrow.

But that's okay. I need all the rest I can get. So does Max, who I assume will be sleeping soundly beside me all night.

But I was wrong.

The bed was empty beside me not long after I drifted off.

My husband was on his way to see that woman.

I just didn't know it.

If I had, then I would definitely have woken up screaming.

HANNAH

Hearing that Max wanted to come and visit me in private certainly caused my heart to flutter. Now the time is drawing nearer, and I can't keep still. I'm pacing around the kitchen in this empty house with soft, slow music playing on my phone, hoping that will help set the mood a little when my man gets here. I've also dressed for the occasion, wearing nothing but my dressing gown, which I hope will make Max curious as to what could be underneath it.

I've been waiting for this moment for a long time. Me. Max. And nobody else.

I'm sure he's coming here just to talk.

But we'll see about that.

It's gone midnight by the time I hear the knock on the door, and while it's late, I'd feared it might have been even later when he called by. He told me that he was going to wait for Nadine to fall asleep before visiting me, but I had been prepared to stay up all night if need be. But he's here now, and as I open the door and get a good look at him, I see that he is alone as promised.

His eyes flicker down at my dressing gown, but he tries to pretend like he is all business and clears his throat before asking if he can come inside. I nod my head and let him in, and after closing the door, I can't help but smile to myself.

This is actually happening. Max is here.

I'm so close to getting what I want.

'Look, I respect you and your position. But I fear this is getting out of hand, and we need to come to some sort of arrangement quickly, for all our sakes.'

Max is wasting no time trying to find a resolution, but after waiting so long for him to turn up here, he can wait for me now.

'How about a drink?' I ask him as I walk into the kitchen, my loosely fastened dressing gown flowing behind me and revealing a little more of my bare legs.

'I can't stay long. Nadine might wake up. She can't know I came here.'

'She won't know. She won't look for you here. I only gave my address to you, not her.'

I wink at the nervous man as he joins me in the kitchen, where the music is now audible, and he can also see the bottle of red wine sitting on the breakfast bar. I picked it up from a corner shop on my way home, and while I'm already a little tipsy from the cocktails I had at *San Bella*, I'm in the mood for more drinks tonight, only this time, I have some company.

'I don't have any glasses, so we'll have to drink out of the bottle,' I say as I unscrew the cap and put the rim of the glass to my lips.

I make sure to maintain eye contact with Max as I drink, wondering if his imagination is running wild at the sight of me with such a suggestive shape in my mouth. But if it is, then he doesn't comment on it. Instead, he notes how sparse the interior of this place is.

'Have you just moved in?'

'No, I've been here a while, actually. I just don't have much stuff.'

'I didn't realise waitresses were so well paid.'

'It's only a house.'

'A pretty big one.'

I shrug before holding out the bottle for him to take. But he doesn't.

'Is this why you turned down my offer of money? You already have enough of it?'

Max obviously thinks that me being in this house is evidence that I am far better off financially than my job would suggest. Of course, he has no idea how and why I am really here. If he did, I'm sure he would be running for the front door. But that's the last thing I want him to do, so I must maintain the illusion if it helps keep him here.

'I inherited this place,' I tell him as I lean back against the breakfast bar and widen my arms behind me, making sure to stretch open my dressing gown a little more as I do. 'I'm not rich, nor do I aspire to be. I meant what I said at the restaurant. I want love, not money.'

Max is having a hard time keeping his eyes off my chest, and it seems his solution to that problem is to turn away from me and pretend like he is more interested in looking out of the dark window.

'If it's love you want, then you are going about it the wrong way. Blackmail. Threats. That's not the way to make people like you.'

'I just had to get your attention. How else were you going to notice me?'

'You think I hadn't noticed you?'

'Had you?'

'Of course. You're the best waitress in that place. And the prettiest.'

'You mean that?'

'Sure.'

I can't tell if Max is being honest or just trying to be nice to knock me off my game, but I'm happy to entertain it for a little while longer because it's lovely to hear.

'I've been in love with you for a while,' I say. 'I've never been able to take my eyes off you. Can you honestly say that your wife's feelings for you are as strong as mine?'

'It's different. We've been married a long time.'

'Different doesn't mean better.'

I wait for Max to look back at me before I put the bottle between my lips again.

'Maybe if I wasn't married, then perhaps something could happen between us. But it can't. I love Nadine.'

'But I'll give you more attention. I'll give you anything you want.'

I open my legs a little then to emphasise my point, and Max can't help but stare at my milky white thighs.

'I can't do it to Nadine. I'm sorry. We have to find some other way of sorting this out.'

It seems we're back at square one again, but I'm not at a complete loss yet. That's because Max is still here with me while his wife is sleeping somewhere else. As long as I have that advantage, then I feel like anything can happen and particularly when I tell him something he doesn't know.

'She's been lying to you. That man she killed was not an intruder. She knew him.'

'What are you talking about?'

'She told me who he was. Do you want me to tell you because I'm guessing Nadine has never told you.'

Max almost looks like he doesn't want to know, but he has to ask.

'Who?'

'He was somebody she had an affair with years ago. He'd found her and followed her and wanted to get back with her. She didn't want that, so she panicked. That's why she stabbed him. And that's why you are now somebody who participated in a serious crime. You buried the man your wife cheated on you with.'

I hope I haven't been too blunt in delivering the disturbing news, but I suppose there is not really a gentle way of telling somebody their partner has been lying to them.

Max stares at me for the longest time, no doubt trying to tell if I'm lying to him, but I'm not, and it's a relief when he sees that. I know he believes me because he hasn't laughed off my statement and walked out.

'How do you know this?'

'Nadine told me when I first confronted her about the body. I felt like there was more to it than him just being a burglar. I've become better at reading people's lies, you see. I had to become that way after my

195

own partner cheated on me and completely blindsided me.'

'But I don't get why she would tell you?'

'She probably thought it might get her some sympathy. She told me he was being threatening towards her. She thinks she was the victim in all of this. But I don't see it that way. I think she stopped being the victim when she committed adultery. What do you think?'

Max looks like he doesn't know what to think, so I take advantage of his defences being down and move closer towards him. He stays still as I near him, and with the bottle in my hands, I ask him if he would like a drink now.

He doesn't refuse this time, and as he takes a swig, I smile because I feel like this is all working.

Of course, he doesn't make it easy. He says there must be some other explanation, and then when I tell him there isn't, he says he needs to go.

But I don't let him. I just step even closer towards him and tell him that I would never hurt him like Nadine has. I tell him that if he was mine, then I would worship him and be the perfect wife.

And then I prove it.

I prove it by letting my dressing gown fall around my ankles before taking his hand and pulling him towards me.

NADINE

I didn't hear Max get up. That's why it was a surprise for me to roll over and find the bed empty beside me. A quick check on the time tells me it's just after six in the morning, and I can see the first light of the new day filtering through the curtains.

Looking around the bedroom, I am trying to tell if any of Max's things are missing. That would give me some idea as to whether he has already left the house or not. But he shouldn't have. It's a Saturday, so there are no meetings today. He's not much of an early morning exerciser either, so I can rule out the idea of him going for a jog at this time of day. No items of clothing seem to be missing, so I have to assume he is still in the house.

But where? And why isn't he in bed with me?

'Max?'

My call goes unanswered in the otherwise silent house, and I know I won't be able to get back to sleep until this mystery is solved, so I pull back the duvet and get up.

I find my dressing gown quickly and tighten it around my waist as I leave the bedroom and step onto the upstairs landing.

'Max? Are you here?'

I'm still not getting any kind of a response, so I go over to one of the windows and look out over the driveway to see if his car is still here. I'd be worried if it wasn't, but there it is, parked in the place it should be. Max must definitely be here somewhere.

I go downstairs in a hurry, afraid that something might be terribly wrong if Max is home but is failing to answer me. Did he get up in the night and have a fall? Or a heart attack? Even with things as bad as they are at the moment with Kieran's murder and Hannah's threats, losing my husband would easily trump all of those things as being the worst to happen to me this week.

That's why it is such a relief to find Max in the kitchen, sitting at our breakfast bar with a cup of coffee in his hand.

'There you are! I was calling out for you. Didn't you hear me?'

Max doesn't say or do anything other than take another sip of his drink, and that's when I notice that he looks exhausted. Like he hasn't slept.

Has he been up all night?

'What's going on?' I ask him as I approach him and try to touch him. But no sooner has my hand touched his arm than he has pulled away from me.

'Hey! What's wrong?'

'You tell me.'

'What's that supposed to mean?'

Max just stares at me, but it's very disconcerting, and I wish I could read his mind because there is clearly something troubling him deeply.

'What time did you get up?' I ask him, but he just shrugs.

'Why didn't you wake me if you couldn't sleep?' He doesn't answer that one either.

'Max, what is going on? Talk to me!'

That finally gets a response from him, but that doesn't necessarily mean things are better, as I'm about to find out.

'Why did you lie to me? Why did you pretend that man was a burglar?'

'What?'

'The man you stabbed! You knew him, didn't you? And don't lie to me!'

'No, of course not!'

'Tell the truth! Tell me how you knew him!'

'I didn't know him, I swear!'

'Liar!'

Max gets to his feet, and for a moment, it looks like he is about to throw his cup of coffee either at me or the wall behind me. But he doesn't do that, although he's clearly incensed by what he's hearing.

How does he know about Kieran? Hannah must have told him. I should have known she would use that information against me. I was a fool for thinking being half-honest with her could ever work.

'You had an affair, didn't you?' Max says with utter contempt in his voice.

'No, wait, I can explain.'

'Then explain!'

Max's loud voice echoes around our cavernous kitchen and makes me jump. It's hard to believe this house was peaceful only a few minutes ago because now it feels like a warzone.

'Yes, I knew him, and I shouldn't have lied to you about that. But there was nothing going on between

199

us. He was here to threaten me, and I had to defend myself.'

'You mean you had to defend your secret? You didn't want me finding out about your affair. But I know now! Tell me when it started!'

'It was years ago!'

'And you think that makes it any better?'

Max's mood is only getting worse, so I just need to bite the bullet and tell him as much of the truth as I can get away with.

I confess to the affair then. I tell him when it started and why, before quickly moving on to when it ended and the fact that I realised I had made a grave mistake and didn't want to lose what I had with him. I'm trying to phrase it all in a way that might make Max see that it was just a genuine and short-lived mistake and that it should in no way detract from all the happy years we have had together. But that's not really up to me to decide. My husband is the one who has been betrayed, so he can choose how he deals with this.

He can choose to forgive me and stay.

Or he can choose to hate me and leave.

Of course, I've left out the part about Adam not being his son because I know for sure that will be a deal-breaker. Max would never forgive me for that, so he can never know, and that's why I kept that secret from Hannah too. Thank God I did, otherwise my life really would be ruined. But this is still bad even without the full story coming out because no one wants to find out their partner strayed.

'How could you do this to me? And how could you lie to me for all these years?'

'I haven't been lying to you! I just didn't tell you because I knew it would upset you!'

'Damn right, it's upset me! How would you feel if you found out I'd been having an affair behind your back?'

'It was a long time ago, and it was over quickly! It's not as if I've been doing it all throughout our marriage!'

'How do I know that? I feel like I don't even know who you are anymore. You lie so easily!'

'It was one lie!'

'You told me that man was a stranger. I buried him, for God's sake! I could go to prison for the rest of my life for that! And for what? To help you almost get away with killing the man you cheated on me with!'

I feel like I'm losing Max, and there's nothing I can say to bring him back to me. Unless I forget about trying to defend myself and just remind him that as crazy as it seems, we have even bigger problems than this.

'I'm sorry, and I understand if you hate me. But we have to deal with this another time. We still have the problem of Hannah to sort out. She'll go to the police if we don't get rid of her.'

Max falls silent again then, and while it's a relief to not have him shouting at me anymore, it's not much help when he closes himself off from me.

'Max, what are we going to do?'

He still says nothing, so I try and bridge the gap again.

'Please, baby. We need to stick together. We have a family, and we've worked so hard for this life. We can't lose it.'

'Get away from me!'

Max finds his voice again in the worst possible way, and he storms out of the room after shouting at me before grabbing his car keys and heading for the front door.

I try and catch him up and beg him to stay so we can talk this through, but he doesn't listen. He just tells me he needs some space and to leave him alone until he has had time to think, which I don't want to do because it worries me, but I see I have no other choice. It's either let him go or throw myself down on the front of his car and refuse to let him drive away. But I won't do that. He has a right to be mad at me, and I just have to pray that he comes back soon.

The house is silent again as I close the front door and stand by the window to watch Max drive away. But as the sound of his car engine fades, I hear a text message alert behind me.

Looking around in the hallway, I see that Max has left his phone behind in his rush to leave. Picking it up, I check the new message, but it's from a number I don't recognise. But it's the content that is the most disturbing.

Last night was crazy. Thanks for coming to see me xx

Who is this?

Unlocking the phone with the passcode we use on all the other devices around our house like the alarm and the TV, I open the message stream and scroll back, and that's where I find an address.

Max was with someone else last night while I was asleep? He was at this address?

There's one way to find out for sure.

I'm going to go there right now.

HANNAH

What a night. It was wild.

I got everything I ever wanted.

I got my man.

Max might have physically left me, but he is still with me emotionally. I can't stop thinking about him.

The way he looked at me. The way he felt.

The way he kissed me.

It was incredible, as well as a little unexpected. Even in my wildest dreams, I could not have envisioned it going so well. Just getting him to this house by himself was a major achievement, but there had still been so much work to do from there to get him closer to me.

To get him to put his hands on me.

But it worked. Max's stance softened when I told him that Nadine had been unfaithful with the man she murdered, and I took full advantage of his defences being down by making my move and making him mine.

We had sex in the kitchen, right there on the floor beside the open bottle of wine that I had been drinking so suggestively. It was rushed and not as romantic as I would have liked, but that wasn't the point. The point was that I got him to be intimate with me and not his wife. Now I have, I'm another step closer to getting him permanently.

Max didn't hang around for long after we had done the deed, and I can't blame him. While it would have been lovely to snuggle and spoon, he had to go. He had to get back home. But unlike when he had arrived at my place, he hadn't been worried about his wife waking up and discovering him gone then.

He had been more concerned about the fact that his partner had been lying to him, and he was on his way to confront her about it.

I wonder how it went. What did he say to Nadine? What did she say in her defence? And would he have told her what he just did with me? I doubt he has been that honest, but he's not the one in the wrong here. Nadine betrayed him first, so he is free to do whatever he wants in retaliation. He chose to sleep with me. It will surely break Nadine's heart. Too bad she broke his heart first.

I'd love to lie around all day and reminisce on the amazing night I had just had with Max, but I can't do that. I've got a lunchtime shift at *San Bella,* and I need to run a few errands in town before that, so I better get moving. It would be nice to just be able to get dressed and walk out the door, but as always, I have to hide all the evidence of my stay here in case Michael's parents call by while I'm out. I'm just about to get started on doing that when I hear the sound of a car parking at the front of the property, and my breath catches in my throat as I freeze and try to figure out who it could be.

Is it the parents? If so, then I am in serious trouble because there's no way I can get everything tidied away in time before they walk through the door. But it might not be them. It could be anybody. Somebody might have got lost. Somebody might be using the driveway to make a U-turn. Or it could be a postman delivering a letter addressed to the deceased residents, one of those few items of junk mail that hasn't been rerouted since they passed. But I'll only find out if I creep towards the window and peep outside.

When I do, I get my answer.

It's not Michael's parents, nor is it a random passer-by or postman.

It's someone I know well but equally, did not expect to see here today.

It's Nadine.

I have no idea how she got my address, but she is here now, and she is on her way to my front door. What do I do? Hide? Pretend I'm not in? That might save me from some short-term pain, but in the long term, it won't be good to have her out there knowing that I'm here. While she has secrets at her house, I have secrets in this one, and now she is on the premises, she has the chance to find out what it is that I am hiding in my private life.

Nadine knocks loudly on the front door but barely gives me time to answer before she knocks again. Then she calls out to me, and what she says removes all doubt as to whether or not she knows where her husband was last night while she was asleep.

'Open this door right now! I know you're in there, and I know Max was here! What did you do with my husband? Come out here and face me, you coward!'

She's angry, and she has every right to be. But I'm still not sure how she knows. I guess Max must have just told her what he did as a way of getting back at her for what she did to him. But that was a bold move on his part, and why did he have to tell his wife where I lived?

Unless she found the address on his phone by accident. That could be it. Max might not know she is here now. Not that it makes much difference because she is still pounding on my door and still calling me all sorts of nasty names.

I'd love to leave her out there, but I'm terrified of somebody driving past and hearing her because I don't want this house getting any extra attention, so I have no choice but to open the door and face Nadine. No sooner have I opened it than she dives into the house and grabs me by my hair, dragging me away from the door and into the kitchen.

'Get off me!' I cry, but it doesn't make any difference, and Nadine's anger is matched by a surprising strength that actually has me worried for my safety for a few seconds. Things only get worse when I see what she has brought with her.

A knife.

Just like the one she killed that man with.

Is she going to do the same thing to me?

I can't afford to hang around and find out. All I can do is reach for the empty wine bottle that we are passing, the same one that Max and I shared last night. Once I've got hold of it, I swing it towards her, and it smashes against the side of her arm, causing her to cry out as the glass breaks and the shards fall all over the tiled floor.

She lets go of my hair, and that allows me to put some distance between us, but she still hasn't let go of the knife, and that's my biggest concern as I look at the blade that is angled towards me.

'You sad little woman! Yearning after other people's lives! Spying on them! Stalking them! Sleeping with them! Well, this is what you get for meddling with strangers! This is what you get for messing with me!'

Nadine rushes towards me again with the knife pointed at my chest, but I dive out of the way and rush around to the other side of the breakfast bar, thankful for its bulk because it gives me a small measure of security in this otherwise dangerous kitchen.

'You can't get away from me! I'll kill you for what you did! How dare you take my husband! He's mine, not yours! Mine!'

Nadine lunges for me again, but the breakfast bar comes to my rescue, and I can keep evading my attacker as long as it is in between us. But I can't keep running from Nadine all day. She'll catch me eventually. That means I'm going to have to make a run for it. Out of the door and as far as I can go. But I don't want to leave here yet. Not while so many of my things are lying around, ready to be discovered if Michael's parents drop by. But somehow, I don't think Nadine is going to do me the courtesy of allowing me to tidy up before she tries to kill me again.

'I hate you!' the vengeful woman cries as she goes for me one more time, and I decide I have no choice but to make a run for it, heading into the hallway and towards the open front door. But just as I get there, I see another car arriving outside, and this time, I know who it belongs to.

It is Michael's father. He's here. *And he's going to catch me inside.*

'Wait!' I cry just before Nadine can get to me, and when she stops, I let her know that we are no longer alone. The sight of the vehicle parking beside hers is sobering enough to stop her from using the knife now she knows she won't be able to get away with it without there being a witness at the scene.

'Who is that?' she asks me as she lowers her weapon, and I don't see much choice other than telling her the truth so she understands the seriousness of the situation.

'It's the person who owns this place. We need to get out now, or he'll call the police!'

I make a run for the back door then, and Nadine follows me, clearly preferring my way rather than the way that ends in having to answer questions to a police officer about why she is here.

I try to scoop up as many of my possessions as I can while I go, and I think I get most of them, but there is no chance to tidy up. Michael's dad will see that somebody has been living here secretly, and that means I can never come back here. But the fact the front door is open already means the game is up.

I'm homeless now.

But at least I'm still alive.

Sprinting across the back garden, I head for the trees while Nadine chases me. But I'm ahead of her, and once I'm amongst the foliage, I make sure to duck out of view so she can't keep following me.

Using the trunk of a tree to hide behind, I stay in position for a couple of minutes until I know Nadine has gone. I can hear Michael's dad calling out in the back garden, trying to find out if the intruders are still near and telling them that he will find them, whoever they are. But he won't find me. I got out. I've got away with it. But what about Nadine?

Her car is still on the drive. What is she going to do about that?

And what is she going to do now she knows I have things to hide too?

NADINE

My foot is all the way down on the accelerator pedal, and as a result, my car is moving a lot faster than the law says it should be on this road. But this is not the time for sticking to the speed limit. All I am interested in is getting away from that house and that man who clearly did not expect to find anybody there.

It was a shock to hear from Hannah that we had to run, and all I could deduce from it was that she was not supposed to be there and had been living there in secret. What made the whole moment even more confusing was I had been hell-bent on killing her only a few seconds before. But that 'plan' had to be shelved in favour of me being able to get away without being caught by the real homeowner, and thankfully, I have made it out. Unfortunately, I lost Hannah in the chaos, but I know I will be seeing her again soon.

She can't get rid of me that easily.

I keep my foot down as I increase the distance between myself and that house, and as I go, I think about how I was fortunate to be able to get to my car and get it out of there before the man called the police. After following Hannah into the back garden, I had been ready to try and hide amongst the trees at the back of the property like she was. But then I had remembered my car was on the driveway, and that meant I wouldn't be able to get away with being there, even if I could hide myself.

Forcing myself to go back, I had hidden around the side of the house as I had listened to the man calling out all sorts of menacing things in the garden before I had been able to sprint around to the front of the property and get back into my car. Then I had high-tailed it out of there, spinning the tyres and kicking up a load of gravel as I got my car on the road before the license plate could be captured by that angry man's phone camera.

I only start to slow down once I'm sure I have got away, and I make the rest of my journey home at a more suitable speed for these roads. It's still early, so I'm grateful for there not being much traffic about, but that's about all I'm grateful for. It's been a hell of a morning. Max confronted me about my affair. I found a suggestive message on his phone. And I visited Hannah at what I thought was her home and chased her with a knife before having to make a run for it myself. That's quite a lot to process at a time when most people in this town haven't even finished their breakfasts yet.

Max is still gone when I arrive back home, but that's okay because I could do without the distraction for the time being. I need to speak to him soon, and I will, but first, I want to find out what the deal with Hannah and that house was.

Why was she there? Who does it really belong to?

And why was she more worried about being caught there than she was about the knife I was threatening her with?

I type the address of the house into my laptop's search engine to see what I can learn from the internet. I'm expecting to have to try and glean some information from things like land registry records and such, and it could take some time. But I'm wrong. All it takes is a split second for the search engine to produce several shocking results.

Once it does, I know everything.

That house is connected to a serious and currently unsolved crime from two years ago when the owners were found dead inside the property. I read every article I can find about Michael and Victoria Spinner, and now I'm thinking of it, their names do seem a little familiar. I must have heard them on the news at the time when the crime was committed. But I had no idea of the full details of the case, nor did I have any idea that the house where the bodies were discovered had stood empty ever since then.

Or so everyone thought.

According to the most recent article I can find online, the property is now owned by Michael's parents, and after finding a photo of the grieving couple in one of the reports, I know now that it was the senior Mr Spinner who turned up and tried to catch us. I feel bad for what that poor man has been through in losing his son and daughter-in-law in such horrific circumstances, but I feel even worse because I have helped contribute to the shock he suffered today when he found out people were inside his son's house when they shouldn't be.

But I know why I was there. I was there to confront Hannah at what I thought was her home. But it's not hers, so why was she there? Did she somehow figure out the house was empty and just decide to start living there rent-free for as long as she could? Or did she know it was empty because she had been there before the murders took place?

More importantly, did she have something to do with them?

Hannah was so afraid when she saw Michael's father arrive that I have to assume she wasn't just worried about getting in trouble for trespassing. She was worried about getting in trouble for something else.

Something worse.

Something like murder.

Could that be it? Could Hannah and I both be harbouring the same secret? We're two killers, and now we both know what the other one is capable of. If so, I need to be more careful than I thought. But this is a good thing. It means I'm not the only one with something to lose anymore. Hannah is as compromised as I am. Neither of us will want the truth to come out. That has to be something we can both agree on. Therefore, it must be possible for us to come to some sort of an agreement.

All I need to do now is see her and tell her what I know.

HANNAH

I hid for half an hour amongst the trees at the back of Michael and Victoria's house as Michael's father looked for the intruder he had chased away from his son's home. I only left once I saw the police cars arrive and figured the officers inside them would be conducting a more thorough search of the area around the house in due course. But while I made it away from the scene safely enough, I'm paranoid as to whether or not I removed every bit of evidence that could lead the police to me in the near future.

I think I got it all. My work uniform. My phone. My I.D. All I left behind was the pillow, duvet and a broken bottle of wine. It's obvious that someone was there, but they shouldn't be able to figure out it was me.

After dealing with my first problem of getting away, I'm going to have to start considering my next problem, and that is where I am going to live now that I have lost my base. I guess a hotel is the most obvious port of call for the time being, but it can't be too expensive because my waitress wage won't stretch that far. It's annoying that I have to find somewhere else, but I guess I was fortunate to be living there for so long for free. I knew it would end at some point. I just wish it hadn't been quite so suddenly and quite so dramatically.

It's crazy to think that being chased around by a madwoman with a knife is not the wildest thing that has happened to me this morning. But being caught by Michael's dad and forced to explain my presence in that home would have been far worse. Depending on how good the police officers' questions were in that interrogation room, they might have been able to make me crack and admit that I knew Michael and Victoria, and once they had done that, I would be a suspect in their deaths. I can't have that because I know I'm not strong enough to stand up to police questioning. I'll crumble because I'm guilty and because the thought of going to prison for the rest of my life feels like a fate worse than death. That's why it's imperative that I stay out of their investigation. As long as they don't know my name and my face, then they won't start digging into my background.

I've spent most of the morning in a bit of a daze, and that's why I lose track of time and almost turn up late for my early shift at *San Bella*. While I do make it to the restaurant in time to start setting the tables for the midday opening, I'm hardly in the best of states when I do. My hair is a dishevelled mess thanks to all the running around; my uniform has mud on it thanks to dragging it through the bushes at the back of Michael's house, and I even have several scratches on my face from a particularly prickly bush that I fell into while I was making my hasty escape.

I'm a mess, and it doesn't take long for my colleagues to notice it.

'What happened to you?' one of the chefs wants to know.

'Are you okay?' one of the waitresses asks.

'For God's sake, go and clean yourself up before we open,' comes the less caring comment from Francesco.

It's only when I lock myself in the staff toilet and look at my reflection in the mirror that I see the toll that the morning has taken on me.

I dab at the scratches on my face with a wet tissue before scrunching up my hair and putting it into a ponytail. The make-up I had to beg to borrow from one of the waitresses allows me to cover up a few of the cuts, and a little water from the tap removes some of the dirt from my white shirt. But I still don't look anywhere near as presentable as someone in my job should look, and I'll do well to get away with just a warning from my employer today.

I spend most of my shift wondering if Nadine is going to show up and demand to speak to me, but that doesn't happen, and I'm grateful for it. She knows exactly where to find me if she wants me, but the fact that she hasn't come looking for me yet hopefully means that she has calmed down. We need to talk sensibly. All three of us. Me. Her. And Max. A lot has happened between us, and this is far from over yet, but there can still be a way for all of us to get what we want, I'm sure of it.

It's also a relief to get through my shift without seeing any police officers turn up and tell me they have a couple of questions to ask me, and by the time I am clocking off and heading downstairs to the staff changing rooms, I am feeling confident that I got away with being at that house.

I undress quickly and change into the t-shirt and jeans I keep in my locker, before bundling my uniform into a small bag and vowing to take it to the nearest dry

217

cleaners before my next shift. With that done, I can focus on leaving here and finding a place to spend the night. But just before I can get out of the restaurant and into the fresh air, I see Francesco coming towards me, and he doesn't look happy, so I wonder if this might be the moment when he gives me that warning about my appearance. I decide to try and pre-empt it by apologising again and assuring him that I won't turn up in such a scruffy state for any of my future shifts. He accepts that apology and says he can forgive me this time because I've never caused him many problems before. But one thing he can't forgive is me not wearing my name badge during my shifts because that's how the customers can identify each waitress, and it makes the staff here seem more personable.

I frown because I'm not sure what he means by that, and I tell him that I did have my badge on because I'm almost positive that I did. But he tells me not to lie to him and warns me not to forget it again before walking away.

Confused, I fish my work shirt out of my bag and check the front of it, expecting to see my gold name badge pinned in the place where it should be.

But my manager is right. The badge is missing. Where is it?

Then it slowly dawns on me what has happened.

I must have left it at Michael's house when I ran. That one thread of evidence that connects me to that place. Not only does it have my name on it, but it has the *San Bella* logo on too, meaning any police officer will easily be able to figure out where it belongs to and call by here to investigate.

This is bad.

This is very bad.

NADINE

My crazy day day took an even crazier turn when I found out that Hannah was connected to a house with a very sinister past. I've been desperate to talk to Max for a couple of reasons ever since. One, because I want to ask him to come home so we can discuss the problems in our marriage, like me having cheated on him and now him having spent the night with his stalker. But two, and perhaps more importantly in the short term, I want to let him know that we might have something we can use against Hannah.

But him leaving his phone at home means I can't reach him. It's frustrating, but I'm not going to spend the whole day banging my head against the proverbial brick wall. I've decided to take action, and I've done so by going to *San Bella* to see Hannah again.

I have no idea what hours she might be working today, but it's early evening, and I expect she will either be just starting a shift or finishing one. That's if she has turned up to work today, of course. After what happened at that house this morning, she might have skipped town. That wouldn't be the worst thing in the world because having her out of the picture should mean that she will leave Max alone and keep my secret about Kieran to herself. But I won't know for sure unless I go and have a look for myself.

I'm about halfway across the car park and headed for the front door when I see Hannah leaving out of a side exit, and just like me, she looks like she is walking with a purpose.

She's shocked to see me when I call out to her, but I hold out my hands to show her that I mean her no harm, unlike the last time we were together and there was a knife between us.

'We have to talk,' I tell her, perhaps stating the obvious.

But Hannah doesn't seem keen on sticking around. She looks in a rush, almost as hurried as she was this morning when she fled from that house.

'I have to go.'

'Why?'

'Because I'm busy.'

'Tell me why you were staying in that house?' I ask her, unwilling to let her leave my sight again until I get some more answers.

'That's none of your business.'

'Your business became my business the moment you threatened me and tried to take my husband. So start talking, or I will, and I've got plenty to say.'

For the first time in a while, it seems I might have the upper hand on Hannah, and she doesn't like it. I'm not surprised because blackmail doesn't work quite so well when the person doing it has as much to hide as their target.

'I was just sleeping there. I knew the house was empty.'

'How did you know that?'

'I just did.'

'Was it because you knew the previous owners were dead?'

Hannah doesn't answer that.

'Tell me. Did you have something to do with their deaths?'

'What? No!'

I laugh because Hannah is a terrible liar.

'You killed them, didn't you? Who were they? Just another couple you were obsessed with? Let me guess, you wanted him, but you didn't get your way, and you killed them both.'

'You don't know what you're talking about.'

'No, I think I do. I think you are even worse than me, and that's why I know you won't go to the police about what I did. It's because you have done something even worse. It's why you ran. You couldn't be caught in that house because the police might figure out you killed Michael and Victoria. But now I know the truth, the question is, what am I willing to do with that information?'

'You won't do anything,' Hannah says rather confidently. 'That's because if you do, then you know I'll tell the police what you did, and we'd both be screwed.'

Hannah might have a point, but at least the balance of power is more equal now. This is much better than when she was holding something over me, and I had nothing to counter with.

'How about we call a truce then? I'll stay quiet, you do the same, and we'll agree to leave each other alone. How does that sound?'

'What about Max?'

'What about my husband?'

'I love him.'

'No, you just love the idea of having a man who might love you. But it's not happening with him. You're going to have to find somebody else.'

'We slept together.'

'I gathered that.'

'And you're willing to forgive him?'

'Yes. And I hope he will forgive me, then we can both move on. I want my marriage to work. That's what real love is, not whatever fairytale you concoct in your head when you're busy watching people from a distance.'

Hannah still seems a little unsure, but I make it easier for her.

'Stay away from my husband, and we'll stay away from you. If you do that, then neither of us will ever have to speak to the police, and we'll get away with whatever mistakes we have made in the past. Okay?'

Hannah takes a few moments to agree, but what choice does she have? Eventually, she nods her head, and I can then nod mine.

'Goodbye, Hannah,' I say, stopping short of holding out my hand for her to shake but making her know that this is the last time we should ever speak.

She doesn't say anything to me, just turns and walks away across the car park. I keep my eyes on her until she is out of view and then go back to my car, feeling like I have accomplished something. I've taken care of the Hannah situation. Now I just need to deal with Max. He's mad at me for what I did with Kieran all those years ago, but he's no angel now after sleeping with Hannah. Therefore, we are equal too, and I'm hoping that simple fact will mean he will come home, apologise and then allow us to move on.

I drive home, hoping that I'll see Max waiting for me there when I arrive. If so, this crazy day might have a happy ending after all. At least for me anyway. I'm not sure how good things are for Hannah now that she has lost her place to live and her only chance at getting with my man. But I'm not going to feel sorry for her. She got herself into this mess by fixating on me and my husband. She could have just done her job. Been a good waitress. Kept herself to herself. Instead, she had to try and get involved in our lives, and that has led to all of these problems for her now.

I still hate her, but I hope she finds some happiness one day. I wouldn't say she deserves it, but her finding some other guy to lust after will at least stop her coming back for Max. I pity whatever poor couple she latches on to next, but there's not much I can do about that. They'll just have to deal with her in their own way if and when the time comes. As for me, I feel like everything is going to work out for the best.

I've got away with adultery. I've got away with murder. And I've got away with dealing with a very dangerous woman who has killed just like me. I'd say I should quit while I'm ahead. I hope Hannah has the sense to do the same.

HANNAH

I used the tip money I gained from my last shift at *San Bella* to pay for a night's stay in a hostel in the middle of town. The two hotels I tried to book had no vacancies, and this was my last option, so it will have to do. But as I drop my bag down on the bed that is surrounded by five other beds in this tiny room, it's hard not to feel like I've lost everything.

My place to live.

My leverage over Nadine.

And my one shot of being happy with Max.

My body sinks into the hard, lumpy mattress as I try to lie back and have a minute's peace, but there's not much chance of that in here. Sharing a room with other people might be fun if those other people are your friends, but those I'm in such close living quarters with now are no friends of mine. They are strangers, some backpackers passing through on their way to a big city, others just people down on their luck like I am.

I get chatting to one such person, or rather, they start chatting to me, and I don't have much choice but to engage with them. The woman in her fifties on the bed opposite mine tells me that her name is Ruth and that she is not going to be here for long because her son is going to come and get her, and she is going to go and live in his big house across town. I tell her that sounds nice, and I suppose it does, at least until it becomes clear the woman is delusional and is making things up as she goes along.

It's barely five minutes after she has told me how wonderful her son is that she suddenly gets angry and calls him a terrible name, before saying he should never have married that hussy and that she will refuse to see him again until they divorce. Finding that Ruth isn't the most reliable of narrators, I get confirmation of that after she has left the room to go to the toilet and another one of my 'roommates' tells me that Ruth has been here for weeks and that her son definitely isn't coming for her.

I feel sorry for the woman and whatever is going on in her mind, wondering what series of events set her off so that she would end up in a place like this, paying £15 for a crap night's sleep in a flea-ridden dorm room. But I've got my own tale of woe, not that I can be so open about sharing it as Ruth is, and there's not too much room for sympathy for others when I'm already feeling so lousy about things myself.

I know what I should have done. I should have taken Max's money. The generous offers he made to me. I could have done so much with that money. Got away from this town for a start. Began a new life. A new career. Potential new friends and possible new lovers. Instead, I stubbornly refused to go, clinging on to some hopeless idea that I could ever end up with a man like Max Murphy.

Nadine has it all, but I have the sneaking suspicion that she isn't fully aware of that fact. She takes it all for granted. The family. The house. The car. The money. The companionship. The love. The life that anyone who doesn't have those things would kill for.

Maybe that's what I have to do. Kill for it. Why not? What else have I got to lose at this point? Things can't get much worse for me than being here in this god-awful room, and as Ruth reappears, I almost feel like looking at her is looking into my future. Is that what I am destined to be? A woman of advancing years, forced to live in grotty conditions with no one to help me because nobody cares about me? The only thing I have going for myself is my job, but how many elderly waitresses do you see working in fancy restaurants? Managers want a touch of glamour for their paying customers, and there must come a point when I'd start getting fewer and fewer shifts until I got the hint that I wasn't wanted there anymore. At best, I'd end up in one of those small cafes serving bacon rolls and cups of tea to weary builders, but the wages will be terrible, and nobody tips in those places.

Then there's the manual aspect of the job. Being on my feet all day isn't a problem now but it surely will be as I age. I'd need something that wasn't as physically demanding. But what?

Who wants me?

Nobody.

What about Max? He still might. He did kiss me, after all. It had to mean something. He broke his vows to his wife by being intimate with me, and that must mean he likes me. I doubt he's ever done anything like that before. That would make me special. But special enough for him to leave Nadine for good and whisk me away to a new life, far away from this hostel and *San Bella* and all the people who have pity in their eyes whenever I cross paths with them?

I spend the majority of the evening curled up on my bed and staring at the wall beside me, while fantasising about how all of this could still be alright. The sounds of Ruth chunnering away on her bed, as well as the weird moans and groans that come from some of the other occupants of this room, only makes me grow more determined to do something to better myself. The lights here go out just after nine o'clock because Ruth has told us she has to be up early so she doesn't miss her son coming to get her. But I don't mind the darkness. I stare into it, and it feels comforting. It also makes it easier to visualise what I am going to do. I've already decided that I'm not going to spend the night here after all. There's little chance of sleep in a room like this, but even if there was, I have more important things to be doing.

I'm not going to give up on Max. And I'm not going to let Nadine get away with having it all, while I have nothing. I am going to go and pay them a visit, and when I get there, one of two things will happen.

Either I get what I want.

Or none of us will.

I hear Ruth tutting as I get off my bed and use the light on my camera phone to help me find my shoes. She's clearly not happy about me disturbing her, but I'll be gone in a moment, and I probably won't be back. Unlike her, I am doing something about my predicament rather than waiting for someone else to improve my fortunes for me.

228

The light is bright in the hostel hallway as I step out of my dorm, and I squint my eyes as I go down the stairs and pass through the 24/7 reception, behind which sits the same bearded man who checked me in earlier. He's eating a Pot Noodle and watching a film on his phone. Living the dream. At least he's being compensated for being here. The rest of us idiots have paid for the privilege of being inside this building.

But I'm in it no more. I'm out on the street now and heading for the nicer part of town. The part where the houses have three bathrooms, and some of the bedrooms are not for beds but for storing all the excess clothing that won't fit in the other rooms. The part where the cars on the driveways are worth more than most people around here get paid for three years of work. And the part where people tuck themselves into bed at night with a sense of comfort, perhaps checking the stock prices on their phone before they drift off and dreaming of how much money they will make tomorrow, while some in this town sit on street corners and beg for scraps.

I know all too well what it's like to be on the unglamorous side of town. But I also know what goes on in the more affluent areas. Both parts can be just as seedy and sordid, and both contain plenty of things that should be kept secret. The key difference is only one part can afford to keep things secret. They hide behind their security gates and their alarm systems, and their big bank accounts. They shake their heads as they drive past the homeless and roll their eyes when their waitress forgets to bring them their drink. But they're no different, really. Everyone's the same. We're all human.

I could have been Nadine in another life. Married to Max. Raising children. Sipping champagne on a Friday night. And she could have been me. Tired. Desperate. Lonely. She wouldn't want to swap, and why would she? But that was my mistake. I gave her a choice. I offered the option. But the blackmail didn't work, and even worse, it almost cost me my life when she came to kill me.

It's time to do what I should have done from the start.

No more asking.

I'm going to take what's mine.

Nadine thinks we are even now.

But we're not even close.

NADINE

I've spent the majority of the evening preparing a lovely, home-cooked dinner for when Max arrives home. I know it will take a lot more than some delicious food and a glass of red wine for us to repair the damage that has been caused between us, but it's a start. I'm treating tonight as a new beginning for us. Hannah is in the past now, as is Kieran and all those dreadful mistakes, and my husband and I can look forward to a bright future.

Sophie and Adam are off having fun, and it's time their parents did the same.

The prospect of all the money from the sale of Max's business means we could do anything and go anywhere. Buy a holiday home somewhere sunny or even move abroad more permanently. We could rent this house out and make a fortune from letting, or we could sell it and cash in completely. We could travel or stay in one place. Wake up and do whatever we feel like. These last few weeks have been the stuff of nightmares, but now we're in the clear, we can go back to living the dream.

Max arrives home at half-past nine, and I greet him with a hug, which is an early test to see how receptive he will be with me. To my relief, he embraces me tightly before we both apologise for the things we have done and said and agree that we both still love each other and can make it all work in the end.

We're both hungry, so we waste no time in eating, and the wine helps the flow of conversation. I tell Max all about my last meeting with Hannah and how she has agreed to leave us alone. He goes over his moment of weakness with her and even thinks him leaving his phone behind for me to discover was some subconscious act in which he actually wanted me to find out what he had done. I'm not sure about that, but I can see he feels guilty, so I agree with him. Then there is just the topic of Kieran to touch on, but Max still has no idea about the full reason why I killed that man, and as long as that is the case, then we can get past it.

'So what's next?' I ask my husband as I put my knife and fork down neatly on my empty plate. 'What do you want to do when you've sold the business?'

Max takes a moment to think about it before telling me that he wants a break from this place. 'We'll get Christmas out of the way with the kids being home, and then I want some sun,' he says with a sense of purpose. 'I don't care where. Just somewhere new.'

'That sounds good to me.'

We clink our glasses together and finish our wine before retiring to the lounge, where we snuggle up together on the sofa and lose ourselves in a movie. I do my best to keep up with the plot, but I do find myself drifting a little as I watch it, mainly because I can't quite believe everything has worked out so well. It almost seems too perfect. Like I'm missing something.

But am I?

Kieran was a threat, but he has been dealt with, and Hannah was a major problem, but she is gone too. So what else could there be? I guess it's a little residual paranoia left over from the stress of recent events. I'm sure it will pass as more time goes by.

232

I make a concerted effort to focus on the rest of the film, and by the time the credits roll, I have done a good job of freeing up my mind. So much so that I'm able to chat about the movie with Max as we turn off the TV and make a move upstairs.

'I liked the twist at the ending,' I tell him.

'Yeah, I wonder how they came up with that one.'

'Do you think there'll be a sequel?'

'Maybe. We'll have to go and watch it at the cinema if there is.'

'Definitely.'

It's the kind of banal chit-chat that I presume most couples go through after watching something together. But it's exactly what I need because it's a sign that things are returning to some semblance of normalcy around here. Give me boring conversation all day over dead bodies, blackmailing bitches and the looming threat of losing my family, my freedom or even my life.

Max is ahead of me, and he is halfway up the stairs when we hear the knock at the front door. I'm only on the bottom step of the staircase, and I spin around to confirm if I really heard what I thought I did.

But there it is again. Another knock.

'Who would be calling at this time of night?' Max asks.

'I don't know.'

'Could it be Hannah?'

'No, she agreed to stay away.'

'She might have been lying.'

'No, I don't think so.'

Another knock. Louder this time.

'They must know we're here,' Max muses. 'The cars are on the drive, and the lights are still on.'

'I know. But maybe we shouldn't answer it.'

'What if it's the police?'

'Why would it be the police?'

'They might have found out what we did.'

'Don't be stupid. They don't know.'

Yet another knock. Whoever it is, they are persistent.

'What should we do?' I ask Max as we both remain on the stairs, staring at the door.

'I'll answer it,' he tells me, not sounding confident at all but at least making a move in the direction of the visitor.

I step aside to allow him to pass, but I stay close to him just in case there could be trouble here, and we should stick together.

As he reaches out for the lock on the door, I take a deep breath, praying that this will just be something silly like a delivery driver trying to find the right address to drop off a pizza.

It can't be the police, and it can't be Hannah.

Can it?

'Wait,' I say to Max just before he turns the handle. 'Are we sure we should do this?'

HANNAH

I knock again on the front door and wonder why it is taking so long for those inside to answer. I know Max and Nadine are in the house because their cars are here, and I can see lights on inside. They would have turned them all off if they were in bed, so they must still be up. So why aren't they answering?

Do they know it's me?

I've been careful to tuck myself out of view from the various windows because I didn't want them to look out and see me before they had opened the door. Therefore, I'm confident they have no idea I have come back to make one last play to get what I want. But perhaps all the uncertainty of these last few weeks has left the Murphys doubting everything, and they are now choosing to cower in their home rather than answer a few simple knocks on the door.

Another minute passes, in which it becomes even clearer that I'm not going to get an answer from inside the house. But no bother. I will just have to find another way in.

Caring less about being seen now, I walk past the front window over which the curtains are drawn, and make my way down the side of the house, hoping I will have some luck around the back of the property.

When I get there, I find another door, but that is locked too. That leaves me little other option but to break my way in forcibly, and I pick up one of the rocks from the decorative garden feature and aim it at the glass on the back door. Throwing it as hard as I can, I watch as the rock goes straight through, sending shattered shards flying in all directions and making an awful din. But it's done the job.

With the glass broken, I can reach inside and turn the lock on the door.

I wonder what the Murphys made of the sound of the glass being smashed. They might be about to call the police. But I'll find them before they can do that.

'Max! Nadine! Where are you?'

My loud cry goes unanswered, and I'm surprised at how much restraint the couple are showing, considering someone has just broken into their home. They would be well within their rights to confront me and tell me the cops are coming or just do something that would let me know that they are acknowledging my presence. But they aren't doing anything.

The house is very, very quiet.

It's only the sound of the crunching glass beneath my feet that I can hear as I move through the kitchen, but before I leave the room, I take out one of the knives from a drawer.

'Max! Nadine! I just want to talk!'

I hold the knife close as I leave the kitchen and step into the brightly lit hallway, and by now, I'm assuming the couple are upstairs somewhere.

But I'm wrong.

They are down here.

They are in the hallway with me, on the other side of the front door that I spent so long knocking on.

But it's no wonder they haven't been answering me.

Max and Nadine were the perfect couple.
But now they are dead.

HANNAH

The first few hours after discovering Max and Nadine's bodies is still a bit of a blur.

All I remember doing is a lot of walking.

I walked out of that house. I walked down the quiet country lanes that surrounded it. And I kept on walking all around town until the sun came up over it. But I don't remember the specific route, nor did I note anything of interest along the way. I didn't register the places I passed or the few people I saw, or even the sound of the birds in the trees as a new day dawned. I was simply too consumed by the shock of finding out that the Murphys were no more.

I eventually made it back to the hostel to collect my things and check out. When I did, Ruth was there, sitting on the edge of her bed with her bag packed and telling me all the same things about her son as she had told me the previous day. She still believed he was coming to pick her up. But by the time I left, she was at reception, having to pay for another night.

I was able to agree on a long-term stay in a basic bed and breakfast hotel in town, and while it won't leave me much out of my monthly wage from *San Bella*, at least it's my own room and a base from which I can start to try and build my life back from.

As fate would have it, my first shift back at the restaurant after learning of Max and Nadine's deaths is a Friday night.

San Bella is busy as always, but one table remains unoccupied. It's extremely disconcerting to see

Table Six sitting empty by the window, and I make sure not to get too near to it as I work through my shift. It's a relief to see another couple take the table in the end, but I won't be trying to get close to this one. Everything is still too raw, and it will be a while before I open myself up to anybody else.

The police say Max killed Nadine before taking his own life. A murder-suicide. He stabbed her and then hung himself beside the body in the hallway. That's what they believe happened, and it's certainly what it looked like to me when I saw them before the police got there. But could that really be what happened? Or is there more to it than that?

Not according to the detectives who have been investigating it. For them, it's an open and shut case, and the reason it seems so obvious is because of what I now know the police found at Michael and Victoria's house after I had left it. Apparently, they had discovered some of Max's things hidden around the home. Like one of his shirts, which a DNA test confirmed had been worn by him.

What was it doing there? I have no idea. I certainly hadn't put it there. But someone had. Someone who wanted to make it look like Max had been the person using the house and not me.

The police found a note in Max's house on his bedside table, in which he had confessed to the killings of Michael and Victoria. He said he had been having an affair with Victoria when Michael came home and caught them. There was a fight between the two men, and he accidentally killed Michael. Then he panicked and removed Victoria as a witness before leaving the house. The note went on to say that he found out the house was empty, and he had then been using it as a place to carry out his next affair. Who was that affair with?

A waitress from an Italian restaurant, apparently.

I wasn't named in the 'confession' letter, but the fact the police had found my name badge back at the house I had fled from meant they were able to track me down and ask me a few questions. They basically wanted to know if it was true. Had I been having an affair with Max in that house? Confirming so seemed to be all they needed to have him treated as the killer of The Spinners and not me, so I told them what they needed to hear.

Yes, Max and I had been seeing each other secretly. We had been disturbed when Michael's father had turned up unexpectedly and ran away. But Michael's dad had seen the car in the driveway, and he was later able to confirm that it was the same one that was parked in the driveway at the Murphy residence. That seemed to fit in with the story that Max had been there that day.

The confession letter finished with Max saying that he knew his things were going to be discovered at the house he had fled, and he didn't want his wife to find out about the affair. But he also couldn't go on living with the guilt of what he had done to Michael and Victoria, and so he had taken extreme measures. He had killed himself and his wife, and that was the end of it.

What do I think about all of that? Well, I know it's a load of nonsense for a start. Max did not kill

Michael and Victoria because I did. Max was not the one who had parked that car outside their house that day when Michael's dad came because it was Nadine. And there is no way Max would have killed himself or his wife out of guilt or fear because he wasn't guilty of murder, and his wife already knew he had strayed with me. He also had two children who he loved and would never leave behind voluntarily.

That all leads me to think one thing. Somebody killed Max and Nadine, concocted a story for the police to buy and, in the process, got me out of it all.

But who?

This Friday night shift is very different to all my other ones and not just because the couple at Table Six are no longer here. It's because all my colleagues at the restaurant are treating me very differently now they have seen my name in the paper and found out that I am connected to the murder-suicide that is the talk of the town.

The media have portrayed me as some man-eating waitress, and the other waitresses at *San Bella* have been lapping it up. No longer am I the boring Hannah who they feel sorry for. Now I'm suddenly the most interesting person they know, and they all have questions for me, including Becki, who clearly thinks I am cool now and hasn't stopped looking at me all night. I just have to play along with it, and while it is a little awkward, I must admit it is nice to be so popular.

But it's not enough to distract me from the very troubling question I still don't know the answer to.

Who really killed Max and Nadine?

I've been racking my brains, but I still don't have an answer. It has to be someone who cares about me, otherwise why would they go to all that effort to make it look like Max was the bad guy? But who cares about me? I don't know a single soul who would hold open a door for me, never mind fake a murder-suicide and send the police in this town down the completely wrong path.

I try to focus on my work for the next part of my shift and stay clear of Becki and the other gawking employees here. Serving a couple of tables in quick succession, I almost feel like I am doing a good job of keeping myself busy.

'Can I take your plates?'

'More wine?'

'Are you ready to order your dessert?'

My last question is to the man at Table Twelve. Tom. On his own as usual.

He looks up at me, smiles and tells me he would like the tiramisu. Then he tells me something else.

He tells me he loves me so much that he has killed for me.

And then he has a question.

Will I go on that date with him now?

EPILOGUE

TOM

Hannah sees herself as someone who will do anything to get the guy.

But I see myself as someone who will do anything to get the girl.

I've been in love with my favourite waitress for a long time, even longer than she spent obsessing over Max Murphy, the married man at Table Six. I've watched her, I've been pleasant to her, and I've been patient with her. I didn't get angry when she turned down my offer of a date a while ago, nor did I ever feel like giving up and turning my attention to someone else who might have reciprocated my feelings. No, I stayed focused and just realised I would have to work a little harder if I wanted to get the woman of my dreams.

After realising that Hannah was in love with someone else, simply by observing her in *San Bella*, I figured the answer to my problem might lie if I started observing her outside of the restaurant. After seeing her go running out of the restaurant one Friday night after Max had abruptly left seconds before her, I followed her to a lovely house out in the countryside. I observed Hannah creeping up to the property and watched as she peeped through one of the windows. I figured this was where her crush lived, but I got confirmation of that fact when I saw the front door to the house open and Max come out, along with his wife, who I recognised from

San Bella. I also saw that they were carrying something between them.

It was the body of a man.

Oh Hannah, what had you got yourself mixed up in?

I continued to follow Hannah so that I was able to see where she lived, and it was quite the surprise when I saw the property she resided in. It was much nicer than I would have thought a single waitress could have afforded for herself. Alas, I soon discovered it was a house with a dark past, and my only question then was what was Hannah's involvement in the murders that had taken place there before?

It was through observation of her at her 'home' that I saw Max visit her one evening, and I watched on in dismay through one of the windows as the pair had sex right there on the floor. It made me angry, but I knew Hannah was just desperate for some intimacy.

She wasn't at fault.

Max was.

I had figured that Hannah was staying in that house secretly by virtue of her always hiding her things before she left, so all I had to do to end her affiliation with that home was send an anonymous message to the real homeowners after finding out who the property was registered to online. I tipped off Michael's parents that there was activity at their deceased son's home, and sure enough, the father went to investigate. I watched as Hannah and Nadine, Max's wife, made a run for it, and they were interrupted not a minute too late because I had feared Nadine might have killed Hannah if she had been able to get her hands on her. But I had been ready to step in if need be, and thankfully, it never came to that.

After watching Michael's father waiting outside for the police to turn up, I snuck into the house and left one of Max's things that I had been able to steal from his jacket in the cloakroom at *San Bella*, namely his gym card. That was enough to make the police believe that he had been the one using the house and set in motion my plan to make it look like he was the one who had killed the poor Spinners.

I knew their deaths were still unsolved, so I decided to clear the mystery up for the bungling detectives who had failed to find the truth. I went to Max and Nadine's house and killed them both, made it look like a murder-suicide and typed up a very convincing confession letter to be found when the cops came calling.

Hannah had no idea about any of this, of course, but I had a feeling she would be more than happy to play along when the police asked her a few questions. I'd noticed she had left her name badge behind when she had fled from Michael's house, but I knew I could make it look like she had just been his mistress and nothing more. The fact she played that role when questioned tells me she had a hell of a lot more to hide than she was letting on, but I don't care. I know she has her secrets, just like I have mine.

More importantly, I know she is someone who will do anything for love.

I am the same, and that's why I believe we belong together. But I see that Hannah might require a little more convincing yet. She's looking at me like she's horrified at what I have done for her. But I give her time to calm down, and as it sinks in how much the pair of us are alike, she starts to soften.

That's how I got her to agree to go for a meal with me next week.

A real date.

A table for two.

Now we're going to be the perfect couple in the restaurant that everyone else is looking at.

Download My Free Book

If you would like to receive a FREE copy of my psychological thriller 'Just One Second', then you can find the link to the book at my website <u>*www.danielhurstbooks.com*</u>

Thank you for reading *The Couple At Table Six*. If you have enjoyed this psychological thriller, then you'll be pleased to know that I have several more stories in this genre, and you can find a list of my titles on the next page. These include my bestselling book *Til Death Do Us Part*, which has a twist that very few people have been able to predict so far, and *The Passenger*, which became the number 1 selling psychological thriller in the UK in October 2021.

ALSO BY DANIEL HURST

TIL DEATH DO US PART
THE PASSENGER
WE USED TO LIVE HERE
THE BREAK
THE RIVALS
THE WOMAN AT THE DOOR
HE WAS A LIAR
THE BROKEN VOWS
THE WRONG WOMAN
NO TIME TO BE ALONE
THE TUTOR
THE NEIGHBOURS
RUN AWAY WITH ME
THE ROLE MODEL
THE BOYFRIEND
THE PROMOTION
THE NEW FRIENDS

(All books available now on Amazon and on Kindle Unlimited – read on to learn a little more about them…)

TIL DEATH DO US PART

What if your husband was your worst enemy?

Megan thinks that she has the perfect husband and the perfect life. Craig works all day so that she doesn't have to, leaving her free to relax in their beautiful and secluded country home. But when she starts to long for friends and purpose again, Megan applies for a job in London, much to her husband's disappointment. She thinks he is upset because she is unhappy. But she has no idea.

When Megan secretly attends an interview and meets a recruiter for a drink, Craig decides it is time to act. Locking her away in their home, Megan realises that her husband never had her best interests at heart. Worse, they didn't meet by accident. Craig has been planning it all from the start.

As Megan is kept shut away from the world with only somebody else's diary for company, she starts to uncover the lies, the secrets, and the fact that she isn't actually Craig's first wife after all...

THE PASSENGER

She takes the same train every day. But this is a journey she will never forget...

Amanda is a hardworking single mum, focused on her job and her daughter, Louise. But it's also time she did something for herself, and after saving for years, she is now close to quitting her dreary 9-5 and following her dream.

But then, on her usual commute home from London to Brighton, she meets a charming stranger – a man who seems to know everything about her. Then he delivers an ultimatum. She needs to give him the code to her safe where she keeps her savings before they reach Brighton – or she will never see Louise again.

Amanda is horrified, but while she knows the threat is real, she can't give him the code. That's because the safe contains something other than her money. It holds a secret. *A secret so terrible it will destroy both her's and her daughter's life if it ever gets out...*

THE WRONG WOMAN

What if you were the perfect person to get revenge?

Simone used to be the woman other women would use if they suspected their partner was cheating. She would investigate, find out the truth and if the men were guilty, exact revenge in one form or another. But after things went wrong with one particular couple, Simone was forced to go into hiding to evade the law.

Having assumed a new identity, Simone is now Mary, a mild-mannered woman who doesn't raise her voice or get angry, meaning nobody would ever suspect her of being capable of the things she used to do for a living. But when she finds out that her new boyfriend is having an affair, it awakens in her the person she used to be. Plotting revenge, Mary reverts back to the woman she once was before she went on the run and became domesticated. That means Simone is back, and it also means that her boyfriend and his mistress are in for the shock of their lives.

They messed with her. *But they picked the wrong woman.*

THE WOMAN AT THE DOOR

It was a perfect Saturday night. *Until she knocked on the door...*

Rebecca and Sam are happily married and enjoying a typical Saturday night until a knock at the door changes everything. There's a woman outside, and she has something to say. Something that will change the happy couple's relationship forever...

With their marriage thrown into turmoil, Rebecca no longer knows who to trust, while Sam is determined to find out who that woman was and why she came to their house. But the problem is that he doesn't know who she is and why she has targeted them.

Desperate to save his marriage, Sam is willing to do anything to find the truth, even if it means breaking the law. But as time goes by and things only seem to get worse, it looks like he could lose Rebecca forever.

THE NEIGHBOURS

It seemed like the perfect house on the perfect street. *Until they met the neighbours...*

Happily married couple, Katie and Sean, have plenty to look forward to as they move into their new home and plan for the future. But then they meet two of their new neighbours, and everything on their quiet street suddenly doesn't seem as desirable as it did before.

Having been warned about the other neighbours and their adulterous and criminal ways, Katie and Sean realise that they are going to have to be on their guard if they want to make their time here a happy one.

But some of the other neighbours seem so nice, and that's why they choose to ignore the warning and get friendly with the rest of the people on the street. *And that is why their marriage will never be the same again...*

THE TUTOR

What if you invited danger into your home?

Amy is a loving wife and mother to her husband, Nick,
and her two children, Michael and Bella. It's that
dedication to her family that causes her to seek help for
her teenage son when it becomes apparent that he is
going to fail his end of school exams.

Enlisting the help of a professional tutor, Amy is certain
that she is doing the best thing for her son and, indeed,
her family. But when she discovers that there is more to
this tutor than meets the eye, it is already too late.

With the rest of her family enamoured by the tutor, Amy
is the only one who can see that there is something not
quite right about her. But as the tutor becomes more
involved in Amy's family, it's not just the present that is
threatened. Secrets from the past are exposed too, and by
the time everything is out in the open, Amy isn't just
worried about her son and his exams anymore. She is
worried for the survival of her entire family.

HE WAS A LIAR

What if you never really knew the man you loved?

Sarah is in a loving relationship with Paul, a seemingly perfect man who she is hoping to marry and start a family with one day, until his sudden death sends her into a world of pain.

Trying to come to terms with her loss, Sarah finds comfort in going through some of Paul's old things, including his laptop and his emails. But after finding something troubling, Sarah begins to learn things about Paul that she never knew before, and it turns out he wasn't as perfect as she thought. But as she unravels more about his secretive past, she ends up not only learning things that break her heart, but things that the police will be interested to know too.

Sarah can't believe what she has discovered. But it's only when she keeps digging that she realises it's not just her late boyfriend's secrets that are contained on the laptop. Other people's secrets are too, and they aren't dead, which means they will do anything to protect them.

RUN AWAY WITH ME

What if your partner was wanted by the police?

Laura is feeling content with her life. She is married, she has a good home, and she is due to give birth to her first child any day now. But her perfect world is shattered when her husband comes home flustered and afraid. He's made a terrible mistake. He's done a bad thing. *And now the police are going to be looking for him.*

There's only one way out of this. He wants to run. *But he won't go without his wife…*

Laura knows it is wrong. She knows they should stay and face the music. But she doesn't want to lose her man. She can't raise this baby alone. *So she agrees to go with him.* But life on the run is stressful and unpredictable, and as time goes by, Laura worries she has made a terrible mistake. They should never have ran. But it's too late for that now. Her life is ruined. The only question is: *how will it end?*

THE ROLE MODEL

She raised her. Now she must help her…

Heather is a single mum who has always done what's best for her daughter, Chloe. From childhood up to the age of seventeen, Chloe has been no trouble. That is until one night when she calls her mother with some shocking news. There's been an accident. *And now there's a dead body…*

As always, Heather puts her daughter's safety before all else, but this might be one time when she goes too far. Instead of calling the emergency services, Heather hides the body, saving her daughter from police interviews and public outcry.

But as she well knows, everything she does has an impact on her child's behaviour, and as time goes on and the pair struggle to keep their sordid secret hidden, Heather begins to think that she hasn't been such a good mum after all. *In fact, she might have been the worst role model ever…*

THE BROKEN VOWS

He broke his word to her. Now she wants revenge…

Alison is happily married to Graham, or at least she is until she finds out that he has been cheating on her. Graham has broken the vows he made on his wedding day. How could he do it? It takes Alison a while to figure it out, but at least she has time on her side. *Only that is where she is wrong.*

A devastating diagnosis means the clock is ticking down on her life now, and if she wants revenge on her cheating partner, then she is going to have to act fast. Alison does just that, implementing a dangerous and deadly plan, and it's one that will have far reaching consequences for several people, including her clueless husband.

WE USED TO LIVE HERE

How much do you know about your house?

When the Burgess family move into their 'forever' home, it seems like they are set for many happy years together at their new address. Steph and Grant, along with their two children, Charlie and Amelia, settle into their new surroundings quickly. But then they receive a visit from a couple who claim to have lived in their house before and wish to have a look around for old time's sake. They seem pleasant and plausible, so Steph invites them in. And that's when things start to change...

It's not long after the peculiar visit when the homeowners start to find evidence of the past all around their new home as they redecorate. But it's the discovery of a hidden wall containing several troubling messages that really sends Steph into a spin, and after digging deeper into the history of the house a little more, she learns it is connected to a shocking crime from the past. *A crime that still remains unsolved...*

Every house has secrets. But some don't stay buried forever...

THE 20 MINUTES SERIES

20 Chapters. 20 Characters. 20 intertwining stories.

<u>What readers are saying:</u>

"If you like people watching, then you will love these books!"

"The psychological insight was fascinating, the stories were absorbing and the characters were 3D. I absolutely loved it."

"The books in this series are an incredibly easy read, you become invested in the lives of the characters so easily, and I am eager to know more and more. Roll on the next book."

About The Author

Daniel Hurst lives in the North West of England with his wife, Harriet, and considers himself extremely fortunate to be able to write stories every day for his readers.

You can visit him at his online home
www.danielhurstbooks.com

You can connect with Daniel on Facebook at
www.facebook.com/danielhurstbooks or on Instagram at
www.instagram.com/danielhurstbooks

He is always happy to receive emails from readers at
daniel@danielhurstbooks.com and replies to every single
one.

Thank you for reading.

Daniel

Made in the USA
Columbia, SC
08 May 2022